CU00687958

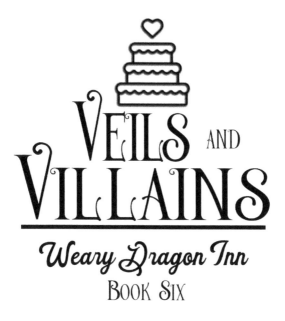

VEILS AND VILLAINS

Weary Dragon Inn

BOOK SIX

S. Usher Evans

Sun's Golden Ray
Publishing

Pensacola, FL

Version Date: 5/6/24

© 2024 S. Usher Evans

ISBN: 978-1945438745

Map created by Luke Beaber of Stardust Book Services
Line Editing by Danielle Fine, By Definition Editing

Sun's Golden Ray Publishing
Pensacola, FL
www.sgr-pub.com

For ordering information, please visit
www.sgr-pub.com/orders

Dedication

To my COVID-cancelled wedding

CHAPTER ONE

"A-*choo*!'

Bev wiped her nose with her handkerchief as bride-to-be Vicky Hamblin whisked by with another bunch of beautiful flowers. Twenty years old, with pinkish skin and dark hair, she had a look of concentration on her face as she dumped the flowers—soft pink with the rest in varying shades of red and white—onto the table.

"Sorry, Bev," she said, surveying the mountain of buds as if they were a puzzle to solve. "I hope to be done with these arrangements soon." She paused, finally looking up at the innkeeper with a scrutinizing glare. "Unless you're getting sick."

"Don't think so," Bev said with a wave. "Just

sniffed one of the flowers wrong, I think."

Vicky sighed, returning to the arrangements. "That's the *last* thing we need. We can't have our innkeeper getting everyone sick right before the wedding."

"I'm fine, I promise," Bev said emphatically, if only to take one source of stress off her plate. "Fit as a fiddle."

Vicky picked up a flower, added another, turned the bouquet, then added more and more until she had a nice bunch in her hand. Bev didn't have a clue what she was looking so hard at the flowers for, but when she was done, the arrangement was quite lovely.

"One down," she said, tying them together and putting them into one of the twenty glass vases sitting on the other table.

"Surely, the lovely woman you brought in can help, can't she?" Bev asked. "What was her name?"

"My wedding planner? Key-ran. Spelled like Karen." Vicky started another bouquet.

Bev had thought everything was sewn up, planning-wise, weeks ago, but clearly there was more to be done. "How did you come across her?"

"I put an ad in the paper in Middleburg," Vicky said as she scrutinized her flower arrangement. "They're a big enough town that they have an actual paper, you know. Anyway, several people answered, but Karen had the best resume of the bunch. Can't imagine why she offered to do my wedding, but she said she liked my *energy*." Vicky plopped a second bouquet into the vase. "Whatever that means."

"And what is her exact job?" Bev asked.

"She's here to help me with everything," Vicky said, the third one coming together quicker, as she seemed to have figured out what she wanted in a bouquet. "Right now, she's meeting with Mayor Hendry to discuss the schedule." Vicky stuck her tongue out as she admired her work. "I think that'll do."

"What does Mayor Hendry have to do with your wedding?" Bev asked.

"We're renting the town hall from her, of course," Vicky said. "But Karen says it would be much nicer if we held the reception in a tent out in the town square, so we need to coordinate with the mayor to find the best time to put it up." She paused, sighing. "I should make some garlands. Didn't even consider what I'd need to decorate the tent."

"Right. And what are all these flowers for?" Bev asked. "I thought you only had a few bridesmaids."

She let out a groan. "Don't mention bridesmaids."

"Sorry." Bev didn't want to inquire further.

"These are decorative," she said. "Going to leave a few here at the inn and take the rest to the town hall. They'll sit on either side of the aisle, plus some for the altar."

"Goodness, what a lot of effort," Bev said. "And here I thought it was enough for two people to meet a cleric under the tree and—"

Vicky smacked her forehead, throwing the half-finished bouquet down. "The cleric! Have we heard from him? When is he supposed to arrive?"

She ran across the room to a very thick stack of papers, rifling through them quickly until she found what she'd been looking for.

"Yes, I've already responded to him," she said, more to herself than to Bev. "I can't keep everything straight anymore. Glad Karen's here to take some off my plate." She paused, looking at the papers in her hand. "Bev, would you mind very much if we went over the list again?"

Bev nodded, though this would be the third time today that Vicky wanted to *go over the list*. She opened the guest book, which was already filled out.

"Room one," Bev said. "Ms. Lucy Edelbert. Your mother's older sister."

"Halfway decent," Vicky said. "If such a thing can be said about my mother's family."

"Room two," Bev continued. "Clarice Willowson, Allen's great-aunt on his mother's side, and her grandson Jacob, who's Allen's—"

"Second cousin and best man," Vicky said. "Poor dear. It's the only family he's got left on his mother's side."

"Room three," Bev said, as she'd already gotten the long-winded backgrounds of each person coming. "Karen. Who's already here and moved in."

Vicky nodded. "It was in her contract that I provide lodging. Best to keep her close to the festivities instead of making her travel from Middleburg."

"Room four," Bev continued. "Wallace and Paul Cordell. Your wedding officiant and his husband."

"Who I'm *very* sure I confirmed via letter," Vicky said, patting her book. "They should be coming in the next day or so."

"Rooms five and six," Bev said. "Marion and Nadia Bilensbrook, your mother's eldest sister and her daughter." She paused, clearing her throat. "Are you *sure* you want them to have separate rooms? Couldn't they double up?"

"Absolutely not." Vicky shook her head. "Can you imagine? I'd never hear the end of it. My aunts aren't the sort of people who believe they should share *anything*. Especially Aunt Marion." She shuddered.

"But is it worth all this effort and expense?" Bev said. Vicky'd already paid Bev almost fifty gold coins to reserve the inn for the week. Bev couldn't believe what everything else was costing the couple.

"Absolutely!" Vicky said, proudly putting bouquet number seven on the table and, without missing a beat, starting on eight. "Goodness knows they've always considered themselves *better* than us, especially with my mother marrying 'that farmhand,' as they called my father. I could scarcely believe they'd agreed to lower themselves to come to Pigsend for the event, let alone for the whole week. Suppose they want to nose around and find things to complain about."

Why would Vicky invite them at all if she felt that way about them? Bev thought it better to keep that question to herself.

"In any case," Vicky said, finishing the tenth bouquet, "*this* will be the event of the year here in Pigsend. It all has to go perfectly!" She paused, looking down at the nearly-empty table and the ten vases left to be filled. "Darn it."

"What?"

"I've got to redo all these," Vicky said, rubbing her head. "I made them too big."

"Can't you go pick more?" Bev asked.

She shook her head, dumping the flowers out on the table. "I picked the fields clean this morning."

"Shouldn't you have picked them a little closer to the wedding?" Bev asked. It was in five days, but it still seemed early to be arranging flowers. "They might not be so—"

"I've got this special food from Middleburg," Vicky said, showing Bev a small bag stamped *HM Flores, Flowers and Greenery*. "Guaranteed to keep them alive and beautiful for up to two weeks.

Besides that, the whole week is positively booked from here on out. I've got to help Apolinary finish the dresses, set up the tent, write my vows, assemble the wedding favors…" She kept ticking items off her list before sighing. "Not to mention play hostess to my aunts."

"Well, you know what you're doing," Bev said, lightly. "I'm headed to the farmers' market. Would you like me to grab anything for you?"

She signed mournfully, and Bev decided to leave her to it.

As angst-ridden as Vicky seemed about her impending wedding, the rest of the town was teeming with excitement. Ida Witzel, the butcher who lived across the street, could barely contain herself every time she came over to the inn. Earl Dollman, the carpenter, was grinning as if the two affianced were his own children. And even taciturn Etheldra, who couldn't be excited about anything, had showed a rare smile last night when the topic of the wedding came up.

"Good thing you're done with…whatever you were doing," she'd said to Bev, eyeing her suspiciously.

Good thing, indeed. Last month, Bev had been embroiled in *yet* another mystery, this one set in Lower Pigsend, a secret underground village nearby. Bev's dear friend Merv had gotten in trouble for effectively leaving the back door open, allowing someone to steal the protective talisman that kept the magical citizens safe from the queen. But Bev had been able to prove the existence of a second tunnel, and in the process, uncovered a larger conspiracy in Lower Pigsend. The talisman was recovered before any major damage was done, though the culprit was banished from the village.

Said culprit was walking toward her, a basket of fruit in her hands. She had curly blonde hair, and her now-freckled and tanned face was tilted up toward the sun. To Bev's eyes, she looked absolutely blissful.

"Watch out there, Lillie," Bev said, making sure to call out before Sin got too close. "You're about to get run over."

The pobyd, a magical creature with an uncanny ability in the kitchen, jumped as her eyes shot open in surprise. "Morning, Bev. Sorry. Wasn't looking where I was going."

"I can see that." Bev slowed Sin. "What are you up to today?"

"Just visiting the market," she said, gesturing to the plump strawberries in her basket. "The fruit looked too enticing to ignore. Couldn't get over the smell of it. It's all I can do not to devour them myself. I missed strawberries so much."

Bev nodded, torn between being happy for Lillie's freedom and feeling she should be a *bit* less content after the trouble she'd put everyone through. Their mutual friend Merv, a six-foot mole man with a penchant for knitting, had been absolutely beside himself, and Bev had taken a financial hit due to being absent from the inn for almost a week. But Bev had sensed the pobyd's desperation and offered to help her get back on her feet. In the month since, she'd been an invaluable addition to the bakery, especially as Allen took on more and more jobs to pay for Vicky's wedding demands.

"How's Allen?" Bev asked.

Lillie's smile faded. "A mess. He's scatterbrained and snippy. Every five minutes, he's running down to check on Vicky or talk to Vicky about something and always comes back looking grumpy. He won't let me help him with his wedding cake, either, and keeps practicing his icing skills on test cakes only to throw them in the trash."

"Vicky's the same," Bev said, thinking of the poor woman having to redo her flowers. "I know they'll both be happier when this is over."

"I'm sure." She laughed. "Well, I'll let you get back to it. I've been up since well before daybreak, and I'm eager to test out my new bed. Not to mention, Wilda says she wants me to bring some baked goods for tea."

Up until this morning, Lillie had been staying at the inn, paying Bev a gold coin per night that she'd earned at Allen's. But since the inn was about to be overrun by wedding guests, she'd found a new place to live—with Wilda Murtagh, who seemed very happy to have a baker living in her spare room.

"Have you decided when you're going to see Merv again?" Bev asked.

Lillie's eyes filled with sadness. "No. I'm still… I don't have my courage about me yet. Nor am I sure he'll forgive me for what I did."

"Well, you'll be a few steps along that path if you bring him something sweet," Bev said. "Minus the sleeping potion, of course."

Lillie's cheeks went pink.

~

At the farmers' market, Bev loaded up on asparagus, radishes, rhubarb, and peas, and restocked her garlic and onion stores as well. Eager to help Vicky impress her supposedly-snooty family, she'd gone into Wim's old recipe cards looking for the best dishes she could make with the fresh produce. On the menu over the next few days: beef braised with the wine Vicky had purchased for the wedding, tender cuts of pork covered in bacon with spring peas, and a rhubarb-and-carrot soup that was sure to impress the most discerning of palates. She'd have to make a second trip in a few days to gather ingredients for the wedding feast she'd be preparing. It was, perhaps, the largest crowd she'd ever cooked for, but with some minor tweaks to her winter solstice schedule, she could make it all work.

After she'd finished unloading the produce to her root cellar for safekeeping, Bev headed across the street to put in her meat order for the day. Vellora was in the front today, whistling as she wiped down the counter. The butcher was head and shoulders taller than Bev, with broad, muscular shoulders, pale skin, and blonde hair.

"How's it going over there?" Vellora asked, nodding across the street. "Has the horde arrived?"

Bev chuckled. "Not yet. But Vicky's driving herself mad trying to make everything perfect."

"I remember Ida being the same way," Vellora said. "But on the day of, all those little details fall away, and all that matters is your wife walking down the aisle." Her blue eyes glittered with happiness.

"I hope so," Bev said. "Vicky's put a lot of effort into this."

Vellora whistled. "We're *all* putting a lot of effort into this. She's got us on the hook to roast a pig. Only reason I agreed was she paid me twenty gold coins and said she wanted the same recipe I used for our wedding." She cracked a smile. "It's an old Witzel recipe, Ida tells me. But she's also ordered twenty pounds of beef for you to cook."

"A pig and twenty pounds of beef?" Bev put her hand to her head. "We'll all be eating for months at this rate. Vicky needs to slow down. I can't imagine how she has all this money."

"Allen's been running himself ragged," Vellora said. "Baking all sorts of goods. I saw him loading up a cake at midnight a few days ago to deliver to a farmer near Middleburg. Good thing he's got that new assistant to help run the show."

"Good thing." Bev shook her head. "We're expecting the lot of them tonight. Planning roasted chicken with spring vegetables. Perhaps four chickens? Just to be on the safe side."

"Plus, the rosemary bread, right?" Vellora asked.

Bev nodded. "Vicky's already on edge. I'd hate to see what would happen if I didn't have *that* for her guests."

"She's only got five days left," the butcher replied. "Everything will be better when it's all over."

Bev turned to leave then stopped, glancing back at Vellora. "Where's Ida today?"

"Delivering half a cow to one of the farmers out of town," she said. "Why?"

Bev gripped her hands, not wanting to broach the subject again, but needing to ask before the festivities got underway. "Did you...erm...hear from your commander?"

Bev had recently discovered that a broken amulet she'd found in her herb garden had belonged to a powerful sect of wizards loyal to the defeated king. She'd gotten flashes of a horrible battle, and several of the queen's soldiers had come to town, questioning Bev's mysterious past. Vellora had also been at that battle, and Bev had asked her if she'd known anything. The butcher hadn't, but said she was still in touch with her commander, who'd know more about such things.

It had been over a month since they'd had the conversation about it, and while no more nosy soldiers had turned up in the meantime, Bev was still on edge. It was better to be prepared with the knowledge of who she used to be than to be surprised.

Vellora's eyes darkened for a moment before she shook her head. "Not yet. It's possible he moved, or perhaps died. Maybe the letter got lost in the post."

"Maybe it did." Bev forced a smile. "Sorry I asked."

Chapter Two

The first wedding guest to arrive was Allen's great-aunt Clarice, who was even more elderly than Bev had expected. Her white hair was wispy, gathered in the tiniest of buns on top of her head. The skin around her eyes sagged so much Bev thought it must've been hard for her to see. And she walked leaning heavily on a sturdy cane and the arm of her much-younger grandson, Jacob. The younger Willowson was perhaps twenty, with brown hair, olive skin, and dark eyes set back into his skull. There was something about the way his hair fell on his forehead and the curvature of his cheek that reminded Bev of Allen.

"You must be Clarice," Vicky said, cutting Bev

off before she could welcome the guests. "It's so wonderful to meet you!"

"Good morning, Valerie," croaked the old woman, reaching out to touch Vicky's face as she approached. "You're prettier than Allen said!"

"It's Vicky," Jacob said with a thin smile to his grandmother before turning to Vicky. "Hi. It's nice to see you again."

To her credit, Vicky didn't blink at being called the wrong name, her smile as wide as ever. "Thank you both so much for making the journey."

"Where's the baby?" Clarice asked, looking around.

"No baby, Granny," Jacob said softly. "This is Allen's wedding, remember?"

The old woman turned, a frown overly exaggerated on her wizened face. "You told me there was a baby!"

Jacob sighed and gave her a sideways look before turning to Vicky apologetically. "She's a little senile these days. You know how old age goes, don't you?"

"She's a dear," Vicky said.

Bev broke in to introduce herself and offer the key. "You two are in room four. Unless… Are you sure she can make it up the stairs?

"It'll take her a minute, but she can do it," Jacob said. "I'll go get our things. Granny, why don't you sit by the fireplace? Come on. That's the way."

"Why don't I put on some tea?" Bev said as the

old woman slowly made her way to the chair, guided by her grandson.

But when Bev opened the door to the kitchen, Biscuit the laelaps came marching out. He resembled a dog in shape and snout, but he had a keen nose for detecting magic—and seemed a little *too* interested in Clarice. She didn't seem to mind, letting out a coo and scratching his head as he put his front paws on her thigh, his nose twitching wildly.

"Bev, I don't know if that dog should be here while—" Vicky started then wisely stopped at the look on Bev's face. "Never mind. How about I see to that tea?"

She quickly disappeared into the kitchen.

"He's harmless," Bev said to Jacob, walking over to make sure Biscuit behaved himself. "I'm sure she's got a bit of food somewhere he's interested in. How was the ride in?"

"Long," Jacob said with a sigh. "If I didn't love Allen so much, not sure we would've come, but…"

"Are you her caretaker full time?" Bev asked.

He nodded. "Besides Allen, I'm her only living relative. My father had been keeping an eye on her, but he died in the war, as did my mother, aunts, uncles, cousins…" His lips pressed into a thin line. "I was too young to enlist, or I'm sure I'd be gone, too. They left me with Granny when they went off to war, and I've been with her ever since."

"Goodness me." Bev had seen people who'd been affected by the war, but not to this degree. Allen hadn't ever mentioned he'd lost so many, even if it was aunts and uncles. It certainly put things into perspective.

Biscuit was now licking the old woman's hand, and she was giggling with happiness. "I like your laelaps," Clarice said with an amused smile.

"Dog, Granny," Jacob said with a weary sigh. "That's a dog."

Bev chuckled nervously, not wanting to correct either of them. "Did your family fight for the—"

"Kingside, naturally. Why do you think they're all dead?" He clicked his tongue. "Well, suppose I'd better unload the carriage and get her things upstairs. Room four, you said?"

Bev nodded. "Do you want me to bring the tea to your room?"

A light snore came from Clarice by the fire, and Jacob looked exhausted. "No, leave it for her when she wakes. I'm going to hunt down Allen. I didn't see him across the street. Have you seen him?"

"Not today, no." Lillie had brought over the muffins earlier. "From what I understand, he's got quite the workload, trying to pay for this wedding. He's been taking cakes and muffins all over the countryside. But I'm sure he'll be by this evening for dinner."

Jacob's face was unreadable, but he thanked Bev

for her hospitality before heading out the front door. He returned shortly thereafter with a pair of suitcases, which he deposited upstairs before saying a hasty goodbye and hurrying out the door.

"First one down, eh, Biscuit?" Bev said to the laelaps, who'd curled into a ball by Clarice's feet and was watching the old woman snore with interest. It was, perhaps, entirely possible that she had a smear of chicken grease or beef broth on her fingers, which made her delectable. But more likely, Fernley's family had the same glimmer of magic that she'd had. Whether it was pobyd or something else, Bev didn't know. But the magic seemed to have ended before it reached either Jacob or his second cousin.

Before she could ponder that further, the front door opened once more, and a woman wearing all black swept in, looking like the world was ending but she was *handling* it. Bev had met Karen earlier, and the woman had arrived almost every hour on the hour with the same intense expression. Her eyes, thin like a hawk's, swept the room with an impatient stare before she threw her hands up in disgust.

"Goodness, where is Vicky? It's quite important I speak with her," Karen said. "The mayor and I have come to an impasse on the chair situation in the town hall, and I need her to make a decision!"

"Karen?" Vicky emerged from the kitchen with a kettle and three cups. "Good, you're here, I need—"

"Before you say *anything*, darling, we must away to the town hall. It's imperative we figure this out before we have to change everything!"

From the tone of her voice, Bev might've guessed that the town was in danger of falling into a sinkhole. Vicky put the kettle down on one of the tables and followed her out the door.

"Was that Verbena?" Clarice croaked, snapping awake. "I can't wait to see the baby."

Bev smiled. "Vicky's gone now. Why don't we have a spot of tea?"

After enjoying the tea, and hearing all about the journey, Bev helped Clarice up the stairs to her room, Biscuit close behind. But Bev made sure the laelaps was out in the hall before closing the door, giving him a look that warned him to behave.

Around two, the next guest arrived, a tall, lanky woman with salt-and-pepper hair. Even though it was a warm, spring day outside, she wore a fur stole around her neck, and a long, thick dress made of a rich material. Since she was alone, Bev could only assume it was the younger of Vicky's two aunts, Lucy.

The woman smiled in greeting, though it was somewhere between kind and lofty.

"Ms. Edelbert, correct?" Bev said.

She nodded.

"Very happy to have you here."

Lucy looked around, her gaze lingering on Biscuit for a moment before sweeping back to Bev. "I was *hoping* my niece would be here to greet me."

"She's busy getting things ready for—"

The door opened again, and a woman who looked like a slightly older version of Lucy strolled in, her chest puffed out. Behind her, a younger girl, with tawny skin and corkscrew curls, followed with a bowed head, holding her hands. Like Lucy, their clothes were finer than anything anyone wore in Pigsend, and their necks, ears, and wrists were adorned with all manner of jewels.

"Lucy, darling." The elder, presumably Marion, swept across the room to kiss her sister's cheeks. "You look a mess. Only arrived?"

"Quite," Lucy replied with a thin smile. "You somehow look—"

"Well, that's the benefit of a *carriage*," Marion said, pity in her smile. "We only travel covered, you know. Helps keep the hair in place. It's such a short trip but goodness me, it certainly does do a number on your skin if you're exposed to the elements."

Lucy's smile was weak, and Bev got the impression the younger sister was used to these comments.

"Where is the…ah." Marion's gaze caught Bev's. "Innkeeper?"

"Yes," Bev said. "Bev, at your—"

"Please see to it that our bags are unloaded

quickly," Marion said, smoothing the folds of her dress. "We'll need plenty of time to prepare before dinner this evening. How many courses are we expecting? Will there be before-dinner drinks? Is the attire formal or shall I wear my—"

"I think there must've been some mistake," Bev said, holding up her hands in surrender. Vicky's concerns certainly seemed valid now. "We don't have that kind of inn. You're welcome to wear whatever is most comfortable."

"Oh. I see." Marion's upper lip curled. "Well, I *do* hope there will be *some* kind of meal served this evening."

"Absolutely," she said, nodding politely. "Tonight's menu will be roasted chicken and spring vegetables. Plus the rosemary bread, of course."

"Mm. I see." Marion looked at her daughter, who'd been eyeing the floor with something akin to disgust. "Nadia, dear, why don't you head upstairs and lie down?"

"Are you *sure* we have to stay here?" the younger asked, now eyeing the hearth. "It's quite dirty."

"Oh, it's got charm," Lucy replied, giving Bev a sideways glance. Compared to her sister, she seemed downright pleasant. "It's very obvious this innkeeper's scrubbed it to within an inch of its life. Can only do so much with what you're given, hm, dear?"

Bev, who *had* scrubbed the place to within an

inch of its life the day before, swallowed her comments and crossed the room with three sets of keys. "Vicky's already prepaid for the lot of you. Dinner will be served at six. The ale is on the house, but—"

"Oh, *ale*. Tell me we'll be drinking something more dignified at the wedding, at least," Marion drawled.

"We will," Bev said. "Vicky's ordered wine from Middleburg, so I understand it. I don't believe we've gotten it in yet, but—"

"Then I'll have to seek out my niece and demand she provide something in the meantime," Marion said, picking up the hem of her skirt and walking toward the stairs. "Innkeeper, I do hope you'll be hasty about retrieving our bags and tending to our horse and carriage. Even though there won't be a *formal* dinner, we'll need to freshen up."

Bev swallowed the urge to tell these fine ladies that guests took their own bags up, as a favor to Vicky.

"Will do."

The carriage was not nearly as fine as Marion and Nadia had let on, and the bags were so heavy Bev had to run across the street and ask Ida to help her carry them up the stairs. The butcher, returned from her meat delivery, obliged without complaint, as she had the magically-derived strength of at least four men. While she tended to the bags, Bev focused on their carriage and snooty horse. Sin wasn't too pleased to share the stables, but Bev softened her with a few carrots and a pat on the nose.

"Just a few days of it, old girl," Bev cooed to her. "Hopefully, everyone will relax after a good meal tonight."

She returned to the kitchen, as the meat was about ready for the oven. Her bread, too, needed to be shaped and prepped for its final few hours before baking. As she worked the rosemary-flecked dough, the tension left her shoulders. As frosty as Vicky's aunts were, they weren't the worst sort she'd ever had at the inn. High and mighty were a piece of cake compared to belligerent or nefarious. Even Wallace, the cleric, had been on Bev's bad side, drinking her ale and begging the bard who'd also been snowed in with them to play until the wee hours of the morning. While Bev *had* told Allen how to get in touch with them, she was hoping the cleric might be a bit less fond of the drink on his second visit. Otherwise, she wouldn't have near enough for him *and* the large wedding.

The front door scraped open again, and Bev dusted her hands on her apron. "Let's see who that is, hm?"

Biscuit, who was sleeping by the dormant hearth, lifted his head with concern.

"Oh, it'll be fine. They're probably just looking for a room for the night," Bev said.

But she stopped short. The man standing at the front desk wasn't Wallace or Paul. He was in his mid-fifties, though his hair was still dark, and he wore a queen's soldier's uniform, complete with lots of badges and buttons signifying a great deal of military victories. He carried a small bag that seemed to have a few spare sets of clothes. Something about him struck Bev as wildly familiar, but she couldn't place it.

"Ah, I was expecting to see Wim McKee," he said with a bit of a sideways look at Bev. "You are…?"

"Bev," she said. "I'm the proprietor of the inn. You must've stayed here in the past."

He nodded with an affable smile. "It's been several years. Where did Wim go? Did the old coot finally retire?"

Bev hated to wipe the smile off his face. "He passed away almost four years ago now."

"Oh, I'm so sorry to hear that." He looked genuinely so. "How long have you been here?"

"Six this summer," she said. "And I confess, you do look familiar, but I'm not sure…"

He smiled, and Bev couldn't help but notice he hadn't offered up a name yet. "I grew up here in Pigsend. Have lots of fond memories here. Everything looks the same, except, of course, the dragon fountain seems to have gone." He tilted his head. "Wherever did it go?"

"Eaten by a sinkhole," Bev said, wondering—a little nervously—if he was planning to stay at the inn, or if he was passing through. "The sculptor was about to start reconstruction, but there's going to be a wedding in the next week, and the bride needs the town square for her tent." She paused, glancing down at the book. Wallace and Paul weren't due to arrive until tomorrow, so she could technically give their room to this soldier. "Did you need a room for the night?"

"For the week, if you've got it," he said with a charming smile.

Bev's hopes sank. "Oh, I'm so sorry. But other than tonight, the bride's got the inn fully booked."

He frowned. "Surely, you've got space for a soldier, don't you? Especially one so tired after traveling all the way from Queen's Capital."

There *was* room. At two beds per, there was plenty of space for Vicky's aunts to share a room, or even her aunt and cousin. And as a general rule, Bev didn't really like turning down a queen's soldier, especially one with so many medals—and one who spent time in Queen's Capital. There was enough scrutiny on Bev's past as it was; no need to give any more soldiers cause to dislike her.

"I'm sure we can figure out something," Bev said, after a moment. "The cleric isn't supposed to arrive until tomorrow, I believe. You can take his room for the evening." And she'd have to shuffle the rest of the guests around when they did arrive.

After striking out Wallace and Paul's names, she hovered her quill over the book. "What name should I put down for you?"

"Zed," he said, something in his gaze telling Bev he'd expected her to know him. "I do appreciate it. Still a gold coin per night?" He slapped down the payment. "Don't tell me you've stopped making that rosemary bread. I daresay that was the thing I missed most about Pigsend. That and Fernley's delicious baked goods."

Bev's face twitched. "She passed away, too. Same plague that took Wim."

He nodded, and sadness enveloped his face. "I heard."

A new worry inched its way across Bev's mind. This man, this soldier, seemed a bit *too* familiar with Pigsend, and with Fernley. Was he some kind of long-lost family member of Allen's?

"Well, here's your key," Bev said, sliding it across the table. "Dinner's at six."

He snatched it up and winked at her. "Looking forward to it."

CHAPTER THREE

As soon as Zed was upstairs, Bev hurried across the street to the bakery to tell Lillie, as the pobyd would certainly want to know about the soldier. Allen was nowhere to be found, but Lillie was hard at work, carefully piping icing onto the top of a cake. The whole bakery had been transformed in the few weeks since she'd started working there, with more intricate chocolate work, cleverer flavor combinations, and a larger variety of different cakes, tarts, and pastries.

"Oh, hey there, Bev," she said as Bev walked in the front door. "Allen's gone off to help Vicky with something, poor dear. She was fit to be tied about whatever it was. Something to do with chairs, I suspect." She paused, perhaps reading Bev's face. "What is it?"

"New guest showed up next door," Bev said. "High-ranking queen's soldier."

Lillie let out a breath, the color draining from her face as she put the piping bag down. "Suppose it was bound to happen sooner or later." She chuckled, absentmindedly playing with the bag. "Goodness, maybe I should talk with Ida. She's been through this a few times, eh?"

"Ida's got a bit of magic, not the whole thing," Bev said. "Look, it'll probably be fine. I obviously didn't tell him a thing about you or anyone else in this town. But you may want to keep a lower profile. Rein in the magic a bit."

Lillie nodded at the nearly finished cakes. "To be honest, it's been so nice baking with flour, I haven't really needed to use much magic. And with the wedding coming up, I figured it'd be risky with the new folks in town, so I've been keeping it as clean as I can." She bit her lip, regret slipping across her face. "Goodness. Thanks for telling me."

"Are you going to skip town?" Bev asked.

It wouldn't have been unreasonable. Lillie had no loyalties to Pigsend and was only here because Bev had offered her a place to stay in the immediate aftermath of her banishment. But in the weeks since, Lillie seemed to have made a home for herself and found a tidy living helping Allen in the bakery.

"I couldn't do that to Allen," she said after a moment. "Not after what he's done for me, helping me get on my feet. If I left, he'd have no one to help with all the baking left to be done this week." She swallowed. "I'm sure I can keep my head down. How long is this soldier in town?"

"He says a week. I had to give him Wallace and Paul's room." She snapped her fingers. "Which reminds me, if you see Vicky, please let her know to come chat with me as soon as possible." Bev sighed. "Goodness, five days until the wedding, and things are going awry, aren't they?"

"Hopefully, a small hiccup," Lillie said.

~

Bev returned to the inn, an ear to the front door for the cleric and his husband, in case they decided to arrive a day early. But as dusk fell, she said a small prayer of thanks. Bev still hadn't managed to find Vicky to tell her that her carefully constructed list had been upended by an errant soldier. She hoped, perhaps in vain, that the soldier would change his mind and only stay one night.

At six o'clock, Bev brought out the first plate of perfectly roasted chickens, and the trio of usual diners sauntered through the door. Earl Dollman was the local carpenter, who had rebuilt half the town in the past year. Behind him was Bardoff Boyd, the lone schoolteacher, and a young man with an eager spirit. The last was Etheldra Daws, who could give Marion a run for her money in the cranky old woman arena.

"Evening, folks," Bev said, placing the platter on the table next to the stack of plates. "We've got a full house this evening. Make sure to leave some for everyone."

"I hope you made plenty," Etheldra said, turning her wizened nose up in her usual fashion. "I'm not about to starve myself for the newcomers."

"There should be more than enough," Bev said with a gentle nod.

"Then why are you taking *two* plates?" Etheldra growled at Jacob, who'd queued up behind her.

"My grandmother." He nodded to the stairs. "Didn't want to bring her all the way downstairs again."

"Understandable," Bev said with a smile. "Be sure to take an extra slice of bread up to her."

He smiled gratefully and took the bowls upstairs, earning another judgmental *harrumph* from Etheldra. But before the tea shop owner could say another word, the event planner swept in, somehow managing to look put together and harried at the same time. She made a beeline for the food, almost pushing Etheldra out of the way as she piled it onto her plate.

"Busy day?" Bev asked with a chuckle.

"You know, event planning isn't for the faint of heart," she said. "I swear, I've run back and forth through this town nearly five hundred times today. Really works up an appetite, doesn't it?" She turned to the rest of those gathered. "Is this everyone?"

"No," Bev said with a nervous look up the stairs. Zed hadn't come down for dinner yet, nor had Vicky's relatives. "The cleric and his husband haven't arrived yet, either."

"Oh." Karen took a big bite of bread. "They'll probably be here tomorrow, then. No use in worrying Vicky about it tonight. She's *got* to start getting more sleep, or else all the paint in the world won't hide those bags under her eyes."

"Yes, about that," Bev said, leaning over. "We've had a bit of a hiccup with the rooms—"

"You're the innkeeper, I trust you'll handle it," Karen said, waving her off as she took her bowl upstairs, leaving Bev and Etheldra staring at each other.

"So you're letting *everyone* eat in their rooms, now, hm?" Etheldra asked.

"It is my inn," Bev said with a look that dared the tea shop owner to argue. "And you'd better be on your *best* behavior this week."

Etheldra had the gall to look offended. "Bev, when have I *ever* been anything but nice to anyone staying at the inn?"

Bev could've reeled off multiple incidents, including the interrogation she'd given a trio of travelers the night before, but she settled for a knowing look. "Vicky's already worked up about her wedding, and I won't have you causing more trouble for her."

"Fine." She picked up her plate, now laden with food. "I'll be on my *best behavior*."

"Thank you," Bev said, as movement on the upstairs landing caught her eye. Lucy walked down the stairs, surveying the crowd with a superior expression, before reaching the bottom. She squared her shoulders as she swept toward Bev, her skirts swishing against the floor.

Bev caught Etheldra giving the aunt an equally superior look, and she glared at the tea shop owner in warning before brightening at Lucy. "Good evening. Glad to have you join us. Are your sister and niece coming down?"

"Oh, who knows with those two," Lucy said with a weary sigh. "It certainly does smell divine. Where shall I sit?"

"Wherever you like," Bev said, handing her a plate. "It's self-serve."

She seemed a little taken aback by that but managed to figure it out. "This bread is—?"

"Rosemary," Bev said. "House specialty. We're famous for it. Won an honorable mention at the Harvest Festival last year."

"That sounds—"

The front door opened, and Allen and Vicky stormed in, arguing quietly and looking like they had been for some time.

"I don't know why it's such a big deal," Allen muttered. "It's *one* set—"

"Allen, everything has to be *perfect*," Vicky replied with a glare. "I—"

They stopped short, perhaps remembering that there was an inn full of people here to celebrate their blessed union. Vicky's cheeks colored pink, and she cleared her throat loudly, while Allen's gaze ducked to the floor.

"Well, hello!" Vicky said cheerfully. "So glad to see all of you. Goodness, Aunt Lucy, I didn't realize you'd gotten in already." She crossed the room to greet her aunt with an overly cheery expression. "You look lovely. Haven't aged a day. Thank you so much for making the trip." She turned around, gesturing with a brief, but irate expression to Allen for him to join her. "This is Allen, of course. Allen, my aunt Lucy."

"Charmed, I'm sure," Lucy said.

"Where's Marion and Nadia?" Vicky asked, looking around. "They made the trip, didn't they?"

"I believe they're waiting to make a fashionable entrance," Lucy said with a half-smile. "Though as I understand it, we don't have any wine for dinner."

"We don't?" Vicky turned to Bev, a frown on her face. "Bev, you didn't get wine?"

"Bev *usually* serves ale with dinner," Etheldra said, cutting in before Bev could respond. "I'd think you'd know that, Vicky. Probably should've arranged the wine yourself if—"

"I'm sure I have a bottle at the bakery," Allen said, perhaps sensing the panic rising in his fiancée. "Let me go find it."

He dashed from the room so quickly that Bev could've sworn he was looking for an excuse to leave.

"In the meantime," Etheldra said, raising her tankard, "highly suggest you try the ale."

"I believe Grant was supposed to be going to Middleburg to pick up several cases in a few days," Bev said, with an apologetic smile. "I'm sure Allen will be able to find one or two bottles in the bakery."

"That's good, because Marion—"

As if summoned, Marion swept down the stairs, wearing a dress that sparkled in the low light of the dining room. Her hair was pinned up, and her ears, neck, and wrists were dripping with jewels. Every eye in the room seemed to be on her, and she knew it, too.

"Well, *good evening*, Victoria." Marion's deep voice echoed through the space. "You're looking peaky, dear. Are you getting enough rest? Eating enough?"

Vicky's lip twitched. "Just the stress of the wedding, I'm sure," she replied with more kindness than Bev would've guessed possible. "You're looking well."

"What in the world are you wearing?" Marion asked, gesturing to the simple dress. "Aren't you a seamstress? This is shoddy craftsmanship, my dear, I hope you weren't the one to sew it. If so, you'll need to find another profession."

Etheldra's gaze darkened, and Bev cleared her throat loudly. "Please, Marion, help yourself to dinner."

Marion turned, her perfectly shaped brow rising. "My dear, I don't *eat* fowl. It's bad for the complexion. And you may address me as Mrs. Bilensbrook, if you need to speak to me at all."

"Now, see here—" Etheldra began.

"It's fine," Bev snapped, giving Etheldra a warning look. "Ms. Bilensbrook, I'd hate for you to go to bed hungry. There's an assortment of spring vegetables, too, and a plate of rosemary bread. Please, help yourself to whatever will suit your… erm…complexion." Bev nodded toward the stairs. "Will Ms. Nadia be coming as well?"

"She's quite exhausted from the long journey today," Marion said. "I've sent her straight to bed. We brought along our own provisions, you know. Never can tell what you'll find in these podunk little towns." She glanced around. "I can't help but notice there isn't any wine. Surely, Victoria, you've gotten that sorted, haven't you?"

"Allen is—"

"Ah yes, where is your fiancé?" Marion scanned the room, her gaze landing on Bardoff. "Is it you?"

"N-no," he squeaked, shrinking down next to Earl, who also seemed to be keeping his head down. "No, I'm the schoolteacher. B-Bardoff Boyd."

"Hmph. Glad to see *someone* is educating the youth of this town." She turned back to Vicky. "Speaking of, where is that brother of yours? He should be here as well, shouldn't he?"

"Grant is…uh…"

"Don't say *uh,* dear, it makes you sound simple."

"Grant is helping with the wedding planning," Vicky said, after a moment. "He's been going back and forth to Middleburg for me. Hasn't quite made it back yet."

Based on the way Vicky's eyes darted around, Bev was sure Grant had adamantly refused to come to dinner at the inn. The teenager didn't seem to like most people or things, and Bev could only imagine how he'd react to his snooty aunt.

Marion was undeterred. "You know, Victoria, when Nadia and I attended your second cousin Bernadette's wedding last spring, all these little *details* were taken care of well in advance. It's a shame your mother wasn't here to guide you. But I suppose we must all do the best with what we're given." She reached into her pocket, pulling out a small box. "I'm sure you don't have a lick of jewelry, what with your meager upbringing, and it's not right for a bride to be without *something* shiny."

All the fight left Vicky's eyes as she took the box, opening it to reveal a beautiful, sparkly bracelet.

"Aunt Marion…" Vicky looked up at her, eyes wide. "This is—"

"Now, I'd better not see you pawn that off to anyone," she said, her gaze stern. "That piece has been in our family for generations. Keep it safe and well-maintained, do you understand?"

"Of course." Vicky pulled it to her chest with a smile. "Thank you so much."

"Try it on, will you?"

Vicky slipped the bracelet on, and it shimmered and shone in the light. "It's perfect."

"It's nothing much, but I suppose it will have to do." Marion surveyed the room and seemed to think the crowd beneath her. "I'm going to retire, dear sister. In the morning, Victoria, I'd like you to call upon me so we can have a chat about the wedding and what you have planned."

"Of course," Vicky said. "Are you sure I can't persuade you to stay and have some dinner?"

"No, no, dear." She gave a final, haughty look at the meal before smiling thinly at Vicky. "In the morning, then."

Then, as pretentiously as she'd arrived, she ascended the stairs, and it didn't seem anyone breathed until the upstairs door was shut.

The regulars excused themselves pretty quickly after that, wishing Vicky well. Etheldra even gave Vicky a squeeze of the hand and an affirming smile before departing. Once they were gone, Vicky sat with Lucy, eating a spot of dinner, but her gaze was fixed on the door, presumably waiting for her fiancé to come back. She gave one-word responses as she pushed her food across the plate, until finally Lucy, too, excused herself to go to bed.

Bev had been starting the process of tidying up, but once Vicky was alone, she sat at the table across from her. "How are you, dear?"

"I'm wonderful. It's my wedding week," Vicky said, with another sad glance at the door.

"Your aunts are…interesting," Bev said. "That's a nice gift Marion gave you."

Vicky glanced at the bracelet, and a small smile came to her face. "It's lovely. I'm surprised she gave it to me. It's something that's been sitting at the bottom of her jewelry box for a decade, I'm sure. But…" She sighed, putting her head on the table. "Goodness. What a day."

"I do hate to add to it," Bev said with a wince.

Vicky groaned. "Bev…"

"Nothing to worry about right at this moment," Bev said quickly. "But the cleric and his husband haven't arrived."

"They're not supposed to until tomorrow,"

Vicky said.

"Yes." Bev fidgeted. "However, I did find someone to let the room to…"

Vicky lifted her head in question, but at that moment, Allen burst through the door, holding a bottle in his hands.

"Found it," he said, proudly. "Not sure it's the best thing we've ever had, but it's red and it's from grapes, so—"

The color drained from his face as he lifted his gaze to the landing of the second story to where Zed stood, still wearing his uniform and medals and a proud smile. His gaze was firmly and unflinchingly on Allen—who stared back with slack-jawed shock.

"Hi, son," Zed said with a knowing smile. "It's nice to see you."

CHAPTER FOUR

In the time it took Zed to walk down the stairs, Allen's face shifted from shock to anger to something like a lidded calm. Vicky seemed unsure what to do, looking between them as if torn between welcoming him with an overly gracious attitude, as she had her aunts, and being affronted by his presence, as her fiancé seemed to be.

Zed made it all the way to the front of the room before Allen finally spoke.

"What are you doing here?" he managed with an even tone.

"Here to watch my boy get married," Zed said with a smile, holding out his arms for a hug. "Look at you. Goodness. You're taller than me now, aren't you?"

Allen said nothing, but his knuckles were white as he balled them by his sides.

"Well, I'd hoped for something of a warmer welcome, but I understand there may be some consternation," Zed said, dropping his arms. "I'd love to hear how life's been for you these past few years. And to meet your lovely fiancée."

Vicky looked at Allen, waiting for him to say something, and when he didn't, she cleared her throat awkwardly. "Oh, well. I…um. I'm Vicky. I've heard…" She swallowed. "Well, not much, but a few things about you."

"None of them complimentary, I suppose," Zed said with a chuckle.

That was, perhaps, an understatement. In the few years Bev had known Fernley before her untimely passing, she'd spoken very rarely about Allen's father, and when she had, it hadn't been very nice. From what Bev had gathered, he'd left when Allen was quite young, but Bev hadn't known any more specifics than that.

Based on the uniform, medals, and stature, he seemed to have found his fortune in the service of the queen's army. He carried himself like a soldier used to commanding a legion, and Bev had to wonder why the draw of the military was more enticing than that of his own family.

"Well, you're here. That's a thing," Allen said,

putting the bottle down with more force than was necessary. "I've got to get up early to bake."

And with that, he stormed out.

Vicky looked between Zed and the door and Bev for a few moments before running after Allen, pausing only a moment to quickly tell Zed she was happy to make his acquaintance. The door shut behind them, leaving Zed and Bev to stare at it.

"Allen's father, hm?" Bev said, after a moment. "Why didn't you tell me the truth when you arrived?"

"I wanted to see him first," Zed said, sitting down at the table. His expression was heavier than it had been before as he examined the bottle Allen had left. "Hoped, perhaps, we might start things on the right foot this time. Suppose that was a bit much to ask for, considering the time I've been gone."

And not corresponded. Fernley had said multiple times that she'd never so much as received a letter from Allen's father. Allen had once described him as "town-skipping." What sort of welcome had he expected after that?

"Well." He put down the bottle. "Maybe we should let the happy couple drink the wine. Do you still serve ale here?"

Bev walked to the cask in the corner and poured him a glass. "Here. And help yourself to dinner. I daresay I made too much. Vicky's aunts don't seem to be the eating sort."

"Really?" He chuckled as he rose to make himself a plate. "Who could resist this delicious meal? I could smell it all the way in my room."

Bev cleared her throat. "So that's why you wanted to stay the week?"

He nodded. "I hope that won't be a problem. I do apologize for throwing rank. It might've made the decision easier had I mentioned I was family."

Bev doubted that. "Well, I'll have to discuss a new arrangement with Vicky's relatives in the morning. I'm sure we can figure something out. Plenty of beds. Allen—er…" She cleared her throat. "Probably his assistant Lillie will be by in the morning with pastries."

"Allen's got an assistant, eh? Doing that well?" He looked somewhat proud. "Have to confess I'm a bit surprised. He wasn't the most industrious of children. Never got up on time, had to be told several times to do *anything*. Was worried about him making his way, but he seems to have picked up the mantle from Fernley."

"Took him a bit, but yes, he did." Bev smiled. "He's a good kid. I hope you two can make amends."

"Are you two…close?" Zed asked hopefully.

"You could say that," Bev said. "Got him out of a tough spot a few months ago. I was happy to help, of course. I think he was busy mourning his mother's death and didn't realize his own abilities."

She was careful not to go into too much detail. Before Bev had figured out what he was doing, Allen had been seeking help of the magical variety and had managed to get a bauble with magic like his mother's. That bauble, in fact, he'd turned into an engagement ring for Vicky—a fact his queen-serving father might not like.

Bev made a mental note to make sure Allen had told his fiancée where it had come from, in case she needed to hide it while the soldier was in town.

"I confess, I do know a bit about you," Zed said, after a moment. "You've developed something of a reputation."

"Me?" Bev didn't like the sound of that. "What kind of reputation?"

"Depends on who you ask," Zed said with a chuckle. "Dag Flanigan seems to think you're hiding some sordid history."

"Oh, Mr. Flanigan." Bev tried to look amused and not concerned as she inspected the chicken.

Two months before, buildings had started falling down all over town, starting with Earl's workshop. Bev had, of course, been roped into finding out why, and thanks to a trio of elderly women, had discovered the culprit: young PJ Norris, who was in the throes of shifting into a dragon for the first time. The women, also shifters, had taken him to a safe place and given him a protective talisman to keep him from accidentally sprouting wings again. Dag

Flanigan had been in town at that same time, drawn to the action and nearly pinning PJ as the shifter. But he'd been drawn away by a clever diversion—though Bev had been surprised he'd fallen for it, as experienced as he was.

"Did he ever find what he was looking for?" she asked.

He cracked a smile. "No. And he's hoppin' mad about it. Not like Dag to let a target go like that."

"Dear me. I was so sure he'd catch up with it," Bev said, hoping her face was neutral and passive. "Is he planning on making a return visit to Pigsend?"

"Not that I can tell," Zed said with a shake of his head. "Seems he's gotten his fill of this town for the moment. But he told me to keep an eye out for anything *strange*."

"Hopefully, anything strange leaves the town alone for the next week," Bev said, and meant that sincerely. "The last thing poor Vicky needs is something else making her crazy. She's been running herself ragged for those aunts of hers for weeks now." She paused. "You aren't in town to investigate something, are you? Do tell me now so I can give Vicky a sporting heads up."

He laughed, and it at least sounded good-natured. "No. Flanigan told me about Allen's wedding when we spoke a few weeks ago. I'm technically on leave for the next week. So even if I do happen upon anything, I'm not likely to investigate."

"And what is it you do in the Queen's service?" Bev asked. "Similar to Mr. Flanigan?"

He cracked a smile. "Flanigan works for me."

"That's…surprising," Bev said, after a moment.

"Why?"

"I suppose I considered the bigwigs of Queen's Capital to have grown up there," Bev said, thinking about it. "Amazing that a youngster from Pigsend could rise so fast."

"I don't know about young, but I certainly earned my rank in the war," he said, and some of the happiness left his eyes.

Another thought skittered through Bev's mind. If Flanigan worked for him, did that mean he was also at the dreadful battle Bev recalled? The one she'd asked Vellora to reach out to her commander about?

She didn't want to ask.

"I don't know if Mr. Flanigan told you," Bev said, "but I don't remember much before I showed up in town. Completely blank." She touched her head. "Grateful to Wim for letting me stay and giving me a job."

"He was an ornery old man," Zed said. "He must've really liked you to have done that."

Bev nodded. "If memory serves, it was because I handled Etheldra without either of us losing our temper."

He whistled. "Etheldra's still in town? Goodness, the number of times she kicked me out of her shop." He shook his head. "I'll have to pay her a visit. I'm sure she'll *hate* to see me."

In more ways than one.

Etheldra was one of many folks in town who had a touch of magic about her. Seeing a queen's soldier wouldn't make her happy, either. In fact, Bev couldn't think of a single person who would be happy about his presence.

"I suppose it's my fault," Zed said after a long pause. "I didn't mean for the years to get away from me. Fernley and I didn't part under the best of circumstances, either."

With Fernley's latent magic, Bev could certainly understand why. Did Zed know his wife had a sliver of pobyd magic in her veins?

"Then the war ended, and I got asked to travel the country in search of…special people." He gave her a furtive look.

"I'm familiar," Bev said. "Mr. Flanigan was clear about his line of work."

"And then before I knew it, five years had gone by, and I hadn't seen hide nor hair of anyone from Pigsend. Didn't think it right for me to show up out of the blue, but when I heard Allen was getting married…" He looked at his barely eaten plate. "I hoped it might be the occasion I needed to rekindle our relationship."

"Good luck to you," Bev said with a nod. "He's a good man, your son. I'm proud to call him a friend." She rose, her plate empty. "I've got to get into the kitchen and start cleaning. If you need anything at all, you know where to find me." She smiled. "Have a good night."

The next morning, Bev rose early and exhaustedly set to her chores. She'd been up late the night before, replaying Zed's conversation with her, Allen's look of horror when he'd realized his father was there, and the forthcoming argument with Vicky's relatives over rooming together. She hoped she could trust Zed when he said he wasn't there to cause trouble, but in her experience, she couldn't trust any of the queen's soldiers to mean what they said.

Still, he'd looked earnest when he'd said he wanted to rekindle his relationship with his son. Bev wasn't in the habit of telling people what to do or think, but she did come up with a good speech about why Allen should at least hear his father out. Forgiveness might be a bridge too far, but he should at least have a conversation with the man.

But Lillie was the one to deliver the morning pastries, casting furtive glances around the space as if Zed was about to jump out and arrest her at any moment.

"No one's awake yet," Bev said, taking the basket from her.

"Oh, thank goodness," she said, visibly relaxing. "I confess, I wasn't keen on coming over here, but there's no one else at the bakery."

"Where's Allen?" Bev asked.

"He left around six this morning to deliver some cakes we'd made yesterday," she said. "Hopefully he comes back in a better mood. He about took my head off this morning when I came in the door too loudly. I think we're all going to be happy when this wedding's over."

"It's not the wedding." Bev told Lillie quietly about Zed's true identity, and Lillie gasped in surprise.

"And Allen had no idea he was coming?" Lillie asked, and Bev shook her head. "Goodness. That's probably not the best sort of surprise you want before a wedding."

"Hopefully, the last one," Bev said.

Lillie nodded. "That does put me a bit at ease, in any case. It's not as if Allen's father is here to sniff out magical creatures."

"May still be," Bev said with a look. "So you'll want to keep your magic to yourself."

Lillie patted the basket. "Not a drop in these. Just beautiful blueberries from the farmers' market." She sighed. "But I doubt I'll be lifting my head out of the sugar this week. We've got a full plate. Allen's said yes to every request in a fifty-mile radius, and they all want their goods this week."

They both turned when the front door opened, but it was only Vicky, who seemed disappointed to see Lillie. She plucked a muffin from the basket and sat in the nearest chair. The bride-to-be was wearing a much prettier dress than the day before, and the sparkling bracelet gleamed on her wrist.

"Where's Allen?" Vicky asked.

"Off to deliver some cakes," Lillie said. "He should be back around midday." Seeing the look of hurt on Vicky's face, she added quickly, "I think he was trying to avoid his father. He was in a mood this morning, for sure."

"I bet." Vicky picked a blueberry from the muffins. "These are really good, Lillie. We're so lucky you showed up to help Allen."

"I'm glad I can be helpful," Lillie said with a bright smile. "And I should probably be getting back to it. These pies aren't going to bake themselves." She paused to squeeze Vicky's shoulder. "Hang in there."

Vicky covered her hand and squeezed back. Then Lillie scurried out the door and across the street.

"Are you all right, Vicky?" Bev asked.

"Yes, of course. It's my wedding week." She plastered on a smile so fake it must've pained her to do so.

Bev placed another muffin in front of Vicky. "Maybe you can start on those garlands for the tent. I'm sure that'll make you happy, won't it?"

"Sure." Another fake smile. "If you see Allen—"

"I'll send him your way."

⸺

All Bev's confidence that she'd be able to handle the snooty guests disappeared an hour later as the two aunts made their way downstairs. Vicky had left with Karen to work on the garlands, and Bev had already spoken to Jacob and Clarice, who'd gone back upstairs after a muffin each. Jacob had been similarly annoyed to hear that Allen had disappeared for the day, but Bev didn't press, especially when Marion's voice echoed loudly from above.

Bev decided to come right out with it, hoping the blueberry muffins might soften the blow.

"Share a room? Absolutely not," Marion replied with a sniff. "The room is small and almost uninhabitable as it is. I can't imagine having to share it with another warm body. I'd practically melt away!"

Bev looked at Lucy hopefully. "Then perhaps Ms. Edelbert can share with Nadia—"

"That won't work either," Marion said. "Nadia has taken ill with the traveling. She'll need quiet for the next few days while she recuperates. I daresay she's going to need her strength about her to be Victoria's maid of honor."

"Oh," Bev said with a frown. "I think that's going to one of the Brewer twins."

"No, clearly not." Marion smiled as if the idea were anathema to her. "Victoria has always said her dear cousin Nadia will be her maid of honor. They're family. You must be mistaken."

Bev sensed that she might've said too much, but the conversation ended abruptly as Vicky ran inside, tears streaming down her face. "Where's Allen?" she cried.

"What's going on?" Bev asked. "What's happened?"

"It's the flowers," Vicky said, wiping her eyes. "They're…they're all *dead!*"

Chapter Five

Bev, Marion, and Lucy followed Vicky as she led them back to the town hall and the dead flowers. The poor girl was shaking, pale and wide-eyed, as she stammered about how she'd taken all the precautions necessary to keep them alive. To her credit, Marion didn't give her opinion, and Lucy offered platitudes as Vicky's hysteria grew worse and worse.

"And I know, I *know* they shouldn't have wilted and died already," Vicky said as they walked up the steps to the town hall. "Oh, Bev, what am I going to do?"

"Take a breath, first of all," Bev said, trying to be gentle. Dead flowers weren't worth the heart attack she'd given everyone in the vicinity. "I'm sure we can find more."

Vicky shook her head. "You don't understand, Bev. I picked the fields clean. It took me two whole days to gather all those flowers from the hills around Pigsend. There aren't any more. And now they're *dead!*"

Inside the town hall, a pungent odor permeated the space. The bouquets Vicky had so painstakingly put together (and re-put together) were sitting along the long aisle of chairs in the town hall. Every single flower had wilted and died, leaving a pile of dead petals at their base.

"Well, this is certainly something," Lucy said, picking up a petal before flicking it to the floor.

"I have to say, this environment isn't conducive to flowers," Marion said, looking around. "Barely any light in here. And how in the world are we supposed to see the bride? Vicky, you must reconsider the location."

Vicky didn't seem to be listening, instead staring at her hard work with a sad shake of her head.

"I found the culprit," Karen said, walking up to Vicky carrying a bag. "Did you use this in the flower water?"

"Yes, I..." She blanched, sniffing the bag. "This isn't right. This is salt."

"Salt?" Karen frowned. She inspected the bag, which still read *Flower Food* on the side. "Goodness, they must've bagged the wrong stuff. Mixed up the weed killer and the food. Absolutely ghastly error. I'll be sure to give them an earful next time I'm in town."

"And who are you, dear?" Marion asked, giving the wedding planner a once-over.

"Karen Mayhew, at your service," she said, holding out her hand expectantly.

Based on Marion's expression, it was rare for her to shake hands, but she did anyway, perhaps taken aback by the wedding planner's confidence.

"Your name sounds familiar," Marion said, tapping her chin.

"I'm sure it does," she said with a bright grin. "I'm one of the premier wedding planners in Middleburg. A high society woman such as yourself, you've probably attended several of my weddings." She rattled off a list of names, none of which Bev knew anything about, but Marion nodded appreciatively.

"Well, Vicky is *certainly* lucky to have you here." She turned to the bride, who was gathering the lifeless remains of her hard work. "I take back what I said last night. You're in good hands. Clearly, some of your grandmother Dianne's wisdom skipped a generation and found you, if you had enough foresight to pick this particular planner."

Was that supposed to be a compliment? Luckily, Vicky didn't seem to be listening. She held the rotting flowers, on the verge of tears.

"What are we going to do?" she asked Karen.

"I'll tell you what we'll do," Karen said, her confident voice booming in the space, perhaps knowing she was being judged by two well-to-do women who could potentially get her more business. "Flowers are out. We'll go for greenery instead. Plenty of that to go around, and we can make it look as fine." She beamed at Marion and Lucy, who seemed dubious. "I can make something from nothing, you watch!"

And with that, the wedding planner led Vicky from the room.

"Well, I daresay we shouldn't have worried so much," Marion said to Lucy. "Here I thought we'd need to help her manage all these little details, but she had the foresight to hire a premier wedding planner. We should've come a few days later."

"I'm sure she can still use the help," Lucy said, picking up a flower and examining it. "Imagine, someone from a flower shop sending plant killer instead of plant food."

"Probably an honest mistake," Bev said.

Lucy nodded, but Marion, once again, spoke for both of them. "Our family has *such* a green thumb, you know. My own sunroom in Sheepsburg is overflowing with flora of all varieties, from fruit trees to flowers to ferns and succulents. We're practically in our local shop every week!" She narrowed her gaze at the discarded bag of plant food. "Every one of *our* shops takes their job very seriously, so a mistake like this is unheard of."

"Well, that's why they call it a mistake," Bev said with a small chuckle. "Vicky's so overwhelmed right now. And it seems Karen's got it all figured out, doesn't it? So I think we clean this up and—"

"We?" Marion chuckled. "You, innkeeper. You're more suited to these sorts of tasks."

"What? Sweeping?" Bev barked a laugh.

"That's a dear." Marion was already halfway to the door. "Come, Lucille. There's a tea shop in town that might be worth a visit. We'll have to see what sort of selection they have."

Whether Lucy wanted to go or not, Marion all but dragged her from the room, leaving no space for argument.

"Well, *innkeeper*," Mayor Jo Hendry's voice drawled from afar. She was leaning against the doorframe of her office, her signature red lips quirked in a smile.

"If you think I'm going to clean all this up by myself, you're dreaming," Bev said, after a moment.

Her smile widened. "That's not what I'm thinking. I'm thinking something seems fishy about these dead flowers."

"Oh, come now. It was an *accident*," Bev said, throwing her hands in the air.

Hendry gestured toward the room. "My dear,

you know as well as I do that things don't just *happen* in Pigsend anymore. To me, this looks like sabotage."

Bev put her hands on her hips. "Who in the world would want to sabotage Vicky's wedding? And for what purpose?"

"Oh, I can think of a thousand reasons someone would want to sabotage their wedding." She ticked off her fingers. "Someone in love with Allen, someone in love with Vicky, someone who wants to end the wedding for other reasons, someone who wants to *show off*—"

"Show off?" Bev blinked. "Show off how?"

"That wedding planner," Hendry said. "Seemed awfully interested in Vicky's aunts. What if *she* killed the flowers to manufacture a crisis she could then swoop in and solve, thus proving herself an *adept* wedding planner."

"That's a bit far-fetched, don't you think?" Bev said with a laugh.

"I think it's suspicious," Hendry continued, examining her nails. "The way she *knew* what to do next, how she was *so keen* on introducing herself to Vicky's aunts, who, as I understand it, are high society in Sheepsburg."

"I mean, I believe that's her job," Bev said. "To know what to do when things go wrong. That's why Vicky hired her, I presume."

"Just saying." Hendry straightened, heading

back to her desk. "Might be time to pull out that glowing stick and investigate."

Bev pursed her lips. "Over dead flowers?"

"First, it's dead flowers, then it's something else. I'm only telling you to get a head start so you don't start on the back foot."

Bev sincerely doubted that someone was out to sabotage Vicky and Allen's wedding, but she couldn't shake Mayor Hendry's smug smile. Would Karen cause trouble for Vicky only to swoop in and solve it, to bolster her own reputation? That seemed bad for business—surely a wedding planner would want everything to go smoothly.

Still, it was something to think about.

While Bev did *not* think it her job to clean up the wilted flowers, if she didn't, the task would fall to poor, overwhelmed Vicky, so with a sigh, she headed back toward the inn to retrieve a broom and dustpan. Down the road, Vicky's younger brother Grant was standing off to the side, talking with his two friends, PJ Norris and Valta Climber. Grant was fourteen, with an attitude problem he'd never shaken, and he wasn't Bev's favorite of the trio of teenagers.

That particular honor went to PJ, the dragon shifter Dag Flanigan had let slip through his fingers. He now wore a talisman that kept his magic hidden from prying eyes, as well as stopping him from destroying the city as a massive dragon. Since then, he'd been nothing but helpful, including giving her a hand at the inn while she was stuck down in Lower Pigsend.

"Morning, Bev!" PJ called, waving. "Beautiful day, isn't it?"

"Morning, PJ, kids." Bev crossed the street to speak with them, hoping they might be able to help her clean up the town hall. "How's it going?"

"I'm hiding from my sister and that *awful* planner of hers," Grant said, crossing his arms over his chest. "I swear, every time she sees me, she has me traveling to Middleburg for this and that. 'Grant, go get me this lace. Grant, go get me this bag of rice. Grant, you got the wrong stuff, I need this other thing.'" He scoffed. "About ready to pack it in and disappear somewhere until this stupid event blows over."

Bev could certainly understand his frustration. "Did you hear what happened to the flowers?"

The trio shook their heads.

"Vicky accidentally fed them plant killer," Bev said. "The whole lot are dead. She's off with Karen trying to find a suitable replacement." She hesitated. "Grant, was that one of the things Karen had you get?"

"I mean, it doesn't ring a bell, but she's had me going all over the place," he said with a scowl. "Why?"

Bev tried to come up with a reason that wasn't accusatory, but it seemed PJ could fill in the blanks.

"What? Is there another mystery afoot?" PJ asked, stepping forward excitedly. "Do you need us to investigate? Find some culprit?"

"I'm not sure there's anything sinister going on," Bev said, holding up her hands. "Which is why I'm asking Grant if—"

"I don't know nothing about it," he huffed. "I go where that Key-ran woman tells me to. Don't even have to pay for anything. She's got a tab everywhere over there. I just—" He groaned.

Bev followed his gaze as the very same Key-ran woman marched purposefully toward them.

"Good, I've found you." She ignored the other two and kept her intense gaze on Grant, who looked ready to melt into the ground. "I need you to stay close this week, where I can find you. Your poor sister is up to her eyes in planning, and we don't have time to spare looking all over town for you."

"I'll be sure to be right where you can find me," Grant muttered with more than a hint of sarcasm.

Karen ignored it. "I need you to go to Middleburg to get these things before sundown tonight." She glanced at the sky. "You'll need to leave right away so you can make it in time."

"More stuff?" He sighed, looking at the sky. "Can't you give me one big list, and I'll get it all at once instead of having to go every day?"

"It's keeping you out of trouble," Karen said, showing him the list. "You'll go to—"

"This address," Grant recited, as if he'd done this a million times already. "Tell them it's yours. They'll load up the wagon."

"Do you need one?" Bev asked. "I'm sure Sin could use the exercise."

"Oh, thanks, Bev, but I've got one Grant's been using," Karen said with a too-bright smile. "Now, listen carefully, Grant. You'll need to tell the vintner you're in town three days early to pick up the cases of wine. They weren't expecting to fulfill the order yet, so they may give you a bit of guff, but we need that wine tonight." She cast a sideways look at Bev. "Since there doesn't seem to be any wine at the inn."

"Was there an expectation there would be?" Bev asked. "Because if so, nobody told me. Also, Allen found—"

"Oh, details, details." Karen put on a too-bright smile. "Come on, Grant. Chop, chop."

Grant let out a heavy sigh, turned on his heel, and slunk in the other direction.

"Now, Bev," Karen said, ignoring Valta and PJ, who seemed rooted to the ground. "We do need to discuss some items on the list. Namely, where the clerics are going to sleep tonight. We're expecting them to arrive this evening, of course, and it would be *awful* if there wasn't a room available."

Bev sighed. She hadn't squared that circle yet, had she? "I suppose I'll talk with Marion and Lucy when I head back to the inn. Unless you want to—"

"Oh, no. It's not my area of expertise," she said, waving Bev off. "Besides that, I'm absolutely swamped trying to get everything else righted. Wedding planning isn't for the faint of heart, you know!"

"You've mentioned that," Bev said.

"Chop, chop, Bev, dear!"

Karen swept away, as quickly as she'd arrived, leaving Bev, PJ, and Valta in her wake wondering what had happened.

"I've got to get back home," Valta said, after a long pause. "My folks want me around to help with the peach picking. Our trees are so full, they're practically drooping."

"Yeah, my mom wants me home for lunch," PJ said. "Was there something you needed help with, Bev?"

"Well, if you two wanted to help me sweep up dead flowers, I'd take it," Bev said before glancing around to make sure no one else was on the street. "There was something else though. Did Grant tell you Allen's father's in town?"

They shook their heads.

"He's a queen's soldier." Bev intentionally looked at PJ. "Dag Flanigan's boss, in fact. So if I were you, I'd lay low for the next few days."

"Did he say anything about, erm..." PJ's face turned red, and his gaze darted to his talisman under his shirt.

"No. From what I gather, he's here for the wedding and nothing more," Bev said. "But he's still here. And if he sees anything funny, he probably won't hesitate to arrest someone. Stay away from the inn for the time being."

"Easy to do," Valta said. "Grant's the only one being ordered around. We've barely seen him the past week, what with him going back and forth to Middleburg."

"He doesn't seem..." Bev paused, thinking of what Hendry had said about someone wanting to ruin the wedding. "You don't think Grant's trying to ruin the wedding, do you?"

Valta snorted. "He wants it over, but he doesn't want it to *not* happen."

"He doesn't like Allen, though, does he?" Bev asked.

"I don't think it's Allen as much as it's the fact that once they're married, Vicky's moving out of the apartment," PJ said. "And Grant will have to find a new place to live—and pay for it himself."

Bev frowned. "He certainly hasn't shown any signs of being able to keep a job. He only lasted a few days with Earl. He wouldn't even help me at the inn."

"Yeah, but that was ages ago," Valta said. "Now

the wedding's here, and next week he won't have a place to live. I'm sure that's kind put a fire under his butt to figure something out."

"And he can't really, not with *Key-ran* sending him to Middleburg every day," PJ added.

Bev could certainly understand that. "Well, I know you two will help keep his spirits up. Goodness knows he and Vicky both need that to deal with their aunts." She sighed as the clock rang. "Suppose I've got to get going on cleaning if I want to be back to the inn at a decent hour." She gave them a hopeful smile. "So you can't help?"

They shook their head.

"Well, worth a shot."

CHAPTER SIX

Bev popped by the inn long enough to grab her broom and dustpan—and interested Biscuit in going with her. When they reached the town hall, Biscuit's nose was a bit too focused on the petals on the ground, which gave Bev pause.

"What d'ya reckon?" Bev asked, grateful Mayor Hendry had gone for a walk. "Is there something magical afoot?"

Biscuit sniffed, his tail only wagging with mild intensity.

"Perhaps not, then," Bev said. "What a mess. Better get to sweeping."

She was halfway done when Allen's cousin Jacob walked through the open front doors of the town hall. He stood at the entrance, scanning the room with a frown and barely noticing Bev.

"Morning, Jacob," Bev said, putting the broom aside. "Looking for Allen?"

He sighed, his hands on his hips. "I swear, he's ducking me. I keep running into that assistant of his, and she tells me he's crisscrossing the countryside to deliver goods. But on his wedding week? Why'd he do that? Why not send her?"

"Maybe it's not you he's avoiding, but his father," Bev said. "I'm sure you heard about that."

"Just what he needs," Jacob said. "This whole thing is…"

He didn't voice his opinions, but Bev got the distinct impression Jacob also thought the dead flowers were a sign.

"I'm sure he'll turn up," Bev said after a while.

"What happened in here?" he asked, walking over to inspect the piles on the floor. "Smells… awful."

"Someone mixed up the plant food," Bev said simply. "But Vicky's fixing it. Should be right as rain by the wedding."

Bev was hopeful he might stay and help, but he instead headed for the door. "I'm going to do another lap around town and hope I run into that cousin of mine."

And once again, Bev was left alone, wondering if *anyone* wanted the two to get married besides the happy couple.

After the mess was all swept up, Bev stopped briefly to chat with Ida and put in her meat order for dinner, as well as catch Ida up on the latest gossip. The butcher had a passing interest in Zed's true identity, but was much more interested in spinning theories about the dead flowers. Bev let her speculate, as well as suggest dinner, then headed back to the inn.

But when she opened the front door, Bev was met by a chattering chorus—some of it quite tense. The Brewer twins, Shasta and Stella, along with the seamstress Apolinary, seemed to be having concurrent conversations with Vicky, who looked even more tired than she had when Bev had left her in the town hall.

"Yes, the guipure lace would be fine on the bodice," Vicky said to Apolinary before turning back to the twins. "I told you, I love you both equally. I'm happy to make you co-maids of honor, but—"

"We don't have *time* to make the guipure lace," Apolinary said, cutting her off. "We've got Chantilly, and maybe I can do a bobbin—"

"You *know* I should be the maid of honor," Shasta said, stomping her feet. "Don't you remember how we went to Middleburg that summer?"

"When we were fifteen!" Stella said. "Vicky, *I*

was the one who held your hand after your mother got ill. *I* should be the maid of honor."

"I'm sure I can find some guipure lace," Vicky said to Apolinary before turning hopelessly to the twins. "I don't know what to tell you. Please don't make me decide on—"

"I'm barely able to finish the dress as it is, Vicky."

"You have to decide who can be your maid of honor."

"It's not fair to say we can both—"

Bev put her fingers to her lips and whistled. All four heads turned toward her. "I think that's enough for today. Why don't we give Vicky a moment to breathe?"

"It's fine," Vicky said, waving her off. "Guipure lace, Apolinary. I'll have Karen find some. Or I can send Grant to Middleburg again to get it." She turned to the twins and pointed back and forth as she sang, "Eenie, meeny, miney—"

They opened their mouths in horror. "Vicky, you *know* we hate that!" Stella cried.

"Absolutely dehumanizing," Shasta said with a dramatic gasp.

"Then share the duties or fate decides," Vicky snapped.

"But who'll stand next to you?" Stella asked. "We can't both do it."

Bev put her hand to her chest, feeling for the

poor bride-to-be. She didn't have the heart to tell her that Marion *also* had an opinion about who should be Vicky's maid of honor. "I'm sure if you put your heads together, you can find a way you both have a special moment with her at her wedding," she offered. "One of you could stand next to her, the other could give a speech at the reception?"

They shared a look of surprise then immediately began arguing over who should do which one.

Vicky shook her head. "It's no use. I've been trying to get them to come to a decision for weeks now."

"They've got four days to figure it out," Apolinary said. "But really, back to the lace. I've got the other three dresses to finish, and yours is still bare. Rosie Kelooke came by to inspect it herself—"

"Oh, bother on Rosie. Hasn't she figured out she's retired? I'll handle it," Vicky said. "I'll find the lace and sew it on myself."

"Sew your own wedding dress!" Apolinary gasped. "I'd never hear the end of it. Besides, you're already busy from sunup until sundown. When are you going to have time to—"

"At night, I suppose," Vicky said.

"Why is this lace so important?" Bev asked.

"Because Caroline Mayweather had a dress made of it solstice before last, and I never heard the end of it from Nadia," Vicky said. "And I *know* if I have anything less, they'll be talking about it to all their friends back home."

Apolinary and Bev shared a knowing look, but Apolinary nodded. "Then guipure it is."

The seamstress left after that, as did the twins, who were still arguing over who was going to do what, and Vicky sank into the chair, working on her greenery. It seemed she'd found strands of daisies and was weaving them together in some kind of long chain. It wasn't nearly as bright or vibrant as the flowers that had died, but it would be lovely, nonetheless.

"I can't believe I was so stupid," she muttered to herself. "I should've *known* that was weed killer. It smelled like it! Don't know where my brain is."

"Clearly, your brain is preoccupied," Bev said gently, picking up some of the greenery and following Vicky's lead to braid it. "Are you all right, Vicky? I know your relations are a lot, but is all this effort worth it? Truly? You can marry Allen under a tree like the Witzels did."

"It is." She flashed Bev a smile that seemed forced. "Karen said she saw you bring a broom to the town hall. Did you clean everything up?"

Bev nodded. "Didn't take me long. Was hoping to snag some help from Grant, but he was off to Middleburg again."

"I'm so grateful he's been so helpful," Vicky said. "We fight like cats and dogs most of the time, but he's really put himself forward for me this week."

Bev avoided her gaze as she looped in another strand of daisies. "His friends—Valta and PJ—they're worried he won't have a place to live after the wedding."

"Well, he won't. Apolinary's giving him one month's grace, as I've already paid the rent, but if I'm not living there, I'm not paying for him." Vicky glanced at the diamond bracelet on her wrist. "And to think, I could pay for several years of rent if I sold this thing."

"It was nice of your Aunt Marion to give it to you," Bev said. "She's certainly a character, isn't she?"

"I'm surprised there wasn't a string attached," she said. "She likes to do that, you know. I'm waiting for her to tell me what I have to do in order to keep it. Happy to hand it back if that's the case." She glanced at the gleaming green ring on her finger. "I have enough jewelry."

"Has, erm, Allen told you where he got it?" Bev asked, her voice low.

"Middleburg, so I understand," Vicky said. "Why?"

Bev could've cursed that baker for his cowardice. "Ask him this evening, when you're alone, what it is. Especially with his father mucking about—"

"Why?" Vicky put down the greenery, concern

evident on her face. "Bev, if you know something I should know—"

Bev sighed. She'd already said too much. "Discuss it with Allen. He's the one who gave it to you."

"More secrets." Vicky angrily picked up the next strand and threaded it with more force than was necessary. "Speaking of Allen's *father*, have we told him to find alternate accommodations yet? The cleric and his husband should be arriving soon. Hate for them not to have a place to lay their heads."

"He's quite a high-ranking member of the queen's service," Bev said. "Can't turn him out."

"And? That doesn't give him the right to upend my whole wedding." Vicky shook her head. "You're being awfully cagey, Bev. I don't like it. I have enough to worry about."

"You're right." Bev nodded. "I'll handle the accommodations. I'm not sure I can dislodge Zed, but I'll work it out with your aunts as soon as Wallace and his husband arrive."

Which Bev hoped wasn't tonight.

~

The cleric didn't arrive before the sun went down, which Bev took as a small blessing for herself, even if it would make the bride-to-be more anxious than she already was. But Bev wasn't in a hurry to broach the subject of the rooms with Vicky's aunts again, and if she could push it off another night, all the better.

The menu tonight was her special beef roast with potatoes, carrots, and aromatics, along with another three loaves of rosemary bread. It all smelled divine. Not even Marion would be able to find fault with it.

As the clock struck six, the inn's front room filled with hungry people. Clarice seemed well enough to come downstairs, helped by Jacob who was doting, verging on overbearing. There was a tension in his face that had been there since he'd arrived the day before, and she wasn't so sure it was due to the strain of caring for an aged relative.

The usuals—Etheldra, Earl, and Bardoff—arrived and helped themselves to dinner. Etheldra seemed interested in Clarice, but kept her distance, opting to sit at a different table. Lucy, dressed much more plainly this evening, served herself and gazed at the table a bit forlornly.

"No wine tonight?"

"Grant should be back any minute now," Bev said, glancing at the clock. "I know Karen wanted to make sure you and Marion had your favorite vintage this evening. Shouldn't be too much longer. But the meal will be delicious while you wait."

Lucy seemed to doubt that, but went to join Jacob and Clarice, who introduced themselves, and the trio tucked in to eat. Bev glanced at the stairwell, expecting Marion and Nadia, as well as

Zed, before too long.

She hadn't seen Allen's father since the night before. He'd presumably slipped out while she was gone, or perhaps had spent the day in his room. Bev wasn't in the habit of keeping tabs on her guests, but she couldn't help but feel she should make an exception for him. After all, there were too many people in town Dag Flanigan might've thought magical enough to arrest; there was no telling what Allen's father might think.

At five past, Zed came in, wearing his military uniform as he had the day before. Etheldra's hawklike eyes sharpened and swept to Bev.

"Ah, Zed," Bev said, her voice loud enough to carry. "I hope you've had a good day back in town."

"An excellent one," he said. "Haven't seen hide nor hair of my son, though. If I didn't know any better, I'd say he was avoiding me."

Jacob's attention turned to the other man, and Bev could practically read his thoughts.

"I know he's trying to tie up plenty of loose ends," Bev said. "But I'm sure he and Vicky will be joining us for dinner tonight. Probably just—"

The front door opened dramatically as Karen stepped through, her dark cloak swept around her shoulders. She stood as if bracing against a raging summer storm, arms akimbo and chest puffed out. Her gaze swept the room with an intensity that rivaled Etheldra's, and she pursed her lips.

"Where's the wine?" she demanded of Bev.

"Grant's not back yet, so I imagine," Bev said lightly. "Or else I'm sure I'd be serving it."

Karen let out a *harrumph* of annoyance before turning on her heel and storming out.

"She's certainly a character, isn't she?" Zed said with a low chuckle. "I hear she's helping Vicky with logistics?"

"Something like that," Bev said. "But she's not the most colorful character here, in my estimation."

"Really? Who could be worse?"

Marion chose that moment to arrive. Once again, she'd adorned her ears, neck, and wrists with diamonds so vibrant Vicky's new bracelet looked cheap in comparison. Her dress was a fine material that swished as she walked. Nadia, still pale and drawn, followed her, looking slightly less expensive, but adorned with jewels nonetheless.

Immediately, Lucy rose to greet her sister, a move that almost seemed subservient to Bev.

"Evening, Marion, dear," Lucy said. "How was your nap?"

"Positively *dreadful*. These beds are as hard as rocks, you know. It'll take *weeks* before my back stops hurting."

Marion's gaze swept the room, looking past everyone else until it landed on Zed. Perhaps she'd noticed his rank and medals, or perhaps it was because he was a soldier, but her entire body shifted, and her smile widened.

"I don't think we've been introduced," she said, crossing the room. "Marion Bilensbrook, of Sheepsburg."

"Zed Mackey," he replied, shaking her hand. "Major commander in the queen's service."

"I can tell." She lifted a brow. "You're giving me a run for my money in medals." She paused. "Mackey… Related to the groom?"

"I'm his father," Zed said.

"Oh!" Marion's eyes lit up with surprise. "Well, Victoria never said her soon-to-be father-in-law was someone of such stature."

It appeared Allen's stock had gone up substantially in Marion's eyes.

Before their conversation could continue, Karen walked through the front door, carrying a crate of wine. She set it down on the table as if it were a prize won in battle and pulled a bottle out.

"Fear not, the wine has arrived," she announced to a lackluster response. But she clearly wouldn't be deterred. "Come, come. Let's get out our finest glasses and share this vintage. Bev, fetch me a corkscrew!"

Bev, who'd already set out glasses for the guests, handed them out, and Karen did the honors, divvying up the wine starting with Marion and Lucy, then Zed, and, a little less enthusiastically, the others in the room. When everyone had at least a little wine, she cleared her throat and raised her goblet.

"I would like to propose a toast to the happy couple," Karen said.

"Where is the happy couple?" Zed asked, looking around, holding his glass up.

"I believe they've both retired early after a long day," Karen said. "Got to get their beauty rest, as it were. So if you'll allow me to toast them in their absence." Again, she raised her goblet. "To the happy couple!"

"To the happy couple!"

Everyone took a sip.

And promptly spat it out.

Chapter Seven

"That's the most disgusting…" Marion began, eyes wide in horror.

If Bev hadn't tasted it herself, she would've thought Marion was being ridiculous, but the wine *was* horrifically sour. Undrinkable, in fact.

"There must be some mistake," Karen said, a nervous laugh bubbling from her lips. "I've ordered wine from them for ages, and—"

"Dear, don't trouble yourself," Marion said, putting down her goblet as if the vessel itself were offensive. "You know, sour wine can happen, even to the most *expert* of winemakers. You get a bit of air, a bit of mold, and it ruins the whole bottle."

"But it wasn't the one bottle," Lucy said, eyeing

her glass. "There were two. Both awful."

Karen insisted it was a mistake, and returned to the crate, opening more bottles. But based on the curl of her lip, and the panicked way she grabbed another one, Bev had a suspicion the entire crate of wine had the same taste.

"Well, I suppose it'll be ale tonight," Etheldra drawled, giving Marion what appeared to be a self-satisfied smile. "Hope it doesn't offend your *delicate* sensibilities."

Bev ignored her and crossed the room to stand next to Karen, who was still opening bottle after bottle in search of one that might be salvageable. "What do you think happened?"

"This is... *Something* must've happened on the transport from Middleburg," Karen said, more to herself than Bev. "A whole crate of wine doesn't go bad like this. Maybe..." She pursed her lips. "Goodness, Vicky's going to be so upset."

"What about the other crates?" Bev asked. "How many did you get from Middleburg?"

"Two more, but I fear if this box is ruined, the others will be, too." She groaned as she covered her face with her hands. "What a waste. Suppose I'll have to send that boy back to Middleburg in the morning for more. That's more gold down the drain."

"The merchant should understand. They've sold you a tainted product, clearly," Bev said.

"You'd be surprised at what they consider drinkable," she said with a wry smile. "I've never known them to take back a dud bottle. But maybe they'll be convinced if they taste this stuff." She sniffed the bottle again. "It's positively rancid." She sighed. "I'm going to check the rest of it."

She bustled through the front door. The others, having dispersed from the toast and returned to their meals, worked quickly to devour them, perhaps to wash the taste of the wine from their mouths. Bev replaced the wine glasses with ale tankards, offering a glass to everyone. Marion and Lucy, unsurprisingly, declined, as did Nadia, who'd barely spoken two words. But next to her mother, who seemed to dominate every conversation she was part of, that was perhaps reasonable.

"Oh, yes, there *has* to have been some mix-up," Marion drawled to Zed, while picking at the meat and vegetables on her plate. She seemed to have lost her disdain for everything Pigsend with his arrival, her interest so keen Bev might've guessed she'd had a romantic eye for the soldier. "Lucy and I frequent the vintner all the time. They're quite popular in Sheepsburg. In fact, I *told* Karen she should visit them for Vicky's wedding wine. Really, the best vintages come from our region, if you ask me…"

She continued, lost in her own conversation as Zed nodded politely, and Lucy kept her gaze down on her meal.

"I can certainly see why Vicky's mother left Sheepsburg," Etheldra said, loud enough for her voice to echo.

Marion gave her a sideways look, debating if the comment was directed at her or not, before Zed asked her something and she turned her attention back to him.

Etheldra, perhaps annoyed that Marion didn't take the bait, rose and deposited her empty plate with Bev. "Good luck to Vicky, dealing with this mess. So hard to find good help these days, isn't it?"

"Karen's doing her best," Bev said, watching the door the planner had left through. "I'm sure she's working through every bottle until she finds one that isn't..." Bev sniffed, the scent of the open bottles in the corner still palpable. "Well, destroyed."

"If you ask me," Etheldra said, "the merchant gave the kid bad wine. Bet you the lot was spoiled and they thought they could get away with it. Probably think we're too common to understand fine wine."

"Now, Etheldra," Earl said, also handing his plate to Bev, "I'm sure it was all an innocent mistake. I saw young Grant with the wagon. Maybe it was something he did. You know those kids. They can't really be trusted to do the right thing. You remember, I had Grant helping me out a bit after those buildings fell down. Could barely swing a hammer!"

"Grant's a good kid," Bardoff chimed in with a frown. "Just…erm…well, he's got a little attitude problem. But he's not going to ruin wine like that."

"Not saying he did it intentionally," Earl said. "But who's to say he didn't leave it sitting out in the sun where it spoiled? He doesn't take the utmost care with things, you know."

"I'm sure we'll get to the bottom of it tomorrow," Bev said.

Clarice and Jacob were next to leave, the latter promising he'd be right back down. "Hopefully, Allen's still awake over there."

"If not, I'm sure Karen can help you find him in the morning," Bev said. "Whether he wants to be found or not."

The only ones left were Marion, Zed, Lucy, and Nadia. From the way Marion was carrying on with Zed, Bev would've thought they'd stay up all night with their one-sided conversation, but as the clock struck seven, Marion announced that she and Nadia needed to retire, as the latter was still regaining her strength.

"Was she ill?" Zed asked.

"Oh, no, but the traveling," Marion said. "It does wear on you."

Zed frowned. "Didn't you say you'd traveled from Sheepsburg?"

"Yes, but you know, my daughter's so delicate."

She rested a hand on Nadia's shoulder, who looked more bored than weary. "We really do love Victoria to have traveled all this way for her special day."

"Ah, right, on that subject," Bev said, sensing her opportunity. If Marion was keen to put on airs around Zed, perhaps she might not throw a fit about switching rooms. "We hadn't planned for Zed to stay here, if you'll recall our conversation. Now, obviously, we don't have to worry about it tonight, because our cleric hasn't arrived yet, but—"

"When he does, we'll cross that bridge," Marion said, rising quickly. "Good evening, innkeeper, Zed, Lucy. Come, Nadia. We've got another long day tomorrow, I believe."

Karen returned shortly after the three went upstairs, shaking her head as she carried another two bottles forlornly. "They're all ruined. I suppose I've got to tell Vicky—"

"Tell me what?"

Vicky walked inside, followed by Allen, and once again, tension lined both their faces. Lillie was behind them, perhaps eager to get a spot of dinner after a long day of baking, though her gaze lingered on Zed for a long moment.

Vicky's gaze dropped to the wine in Karen's hand, and she frowned even more.

"Is that the wine Grant brought back from Middleburg?" she asked. "What's wrong with it?"

"It's…erm…" Karen began.

"They're a bit of a dud, son," Zed said rising. "Can't possibly serve this at your wedding."

"That's impossible," Vicky said, rushing forward. "They're…" She sniffed the wine and made a face. "Oh my goodness, how awful. What in the world happened?"

"I don't know," Bev said. "Grant brought them from Middleburg. Maybe they sat out too long in the sun?"

"Probably a mix-up," Karen said, somehow regaining her gumption. "Allen, you should go to Middleburg tomorrow and demand a different case of wine."

"Can't," Allen said, crossing his arms. "We have five batches of cookies to deliver in the opposite direction."

"Then send Lillie to deliver them," Vicky said, her gaze on him. "We can't serve lackluster wine, Allen."

"It's not lackluster," Bev said with a wince. "It's rancid."

Lillie picked up a bottle and inspected it, saying nothing.

"Vicky, there's no more gold in the budget to buy more wine," Allen said, his tone low, as he gave Zed a furtive glance, as if he didn't want him to overhear.

"We can't *not* have wine at the wedding," Vicky said, gesturing to the crate. "Surely, the merchant will see they gave us a shoddy case and gladly give us another."

"Unless they say it was Grant's fault," Allen shot back. "What if it was perfectly fine wine leaving Middleburg, but Grant dawdled too long bringing it back and he ruined it? What then?"

"He didn't *dawdle*," Vicky snapped.

"Didn't he? Left midday, didn't come back until sundown," Allen huffed. "He dawdled. Wasn't he supposed to get the tent up today, Karen?"

"Yes, but we can deal with that tomorrow," Karen said with a wave of her hand. "It's fine. We'll take care of it."

She certainly seemed less unctuous now that Marion was out of earshot, but at least she seemed to be on top of things.

"If money's an issue…" Zed began carefully.

"It's not," Allen shot back.

"Allen, let him speak," Vicky waved him off. "You were saying?"

"I've got some gold I can give you," Zed continued. "Not sure if it'll cover the cost of the wine, but—"

"We don't need your money." Allen glowered. "Not now, and not eight years ago when you left."

"Allen, I—"

"Ahem." Lillie cleared her throat loudly. "Maybe we give the wine a second look?"

Karen scoffed. "Dear, it's *clearly* ruined."

Lillie walked the bottle to Vicky. "Sometimes if you shake it a bit, it loosens up some of the…erm… juice. Airing it out helps, too."

Vicky sniffed it then took a hesitant sip. Relief spread across her entire face. "Oh, Lillie. What've you done to it? I could kiss you!"

"What indeed?" Bev muttered, giving the pobyd a sideways glance.

Lillie's cheeks went pink. "Nothing. Just have some experience with wine, that's all. You've got to move it just so, sometimes. I'm sure the rest of the bottles will be okay, too. We'll put the cork back in, and they'll be right as rain by your wedding." She beamed at the couple. "Not to worry."

"Well, this is a miracle," Zed said, crossing the room. "You're Allen's assistant, aren't you? Lillie, right?"

She nodded, and Bev didn't miss how her gaze swept over Zed's uniform. "I am. Didn't do anything special. Just let it breathe a bit." She took a hesitant step back. "You know, maybe we should keep these at the bakery until the wedding. Bev, do you think you could help me get them back over?"

⁓

"You shouldn't have done that," Bev said, as soon as they were inside the bakery. "Lillie, that was *wildly* dangerous. Right in front of a soldier?"

"I know, I know. But I couldn't stand to see Vicky so upset," Lillie said, picking up another bottle and twisting it in her hand. "Especially when I'm perfectly capable of bringing bad wine back to life. Just a little tweak of the flavoring."

"You used *magic* in front of a *queen's soldier*," Bev said, gesturing back to the inn across the street. "What if he can detect the magic in the wine?"

She paused, looking at Bev as if seeing her for the first time. "How would he do that?"

"They have ways, believe me," Bev said, thinking of that pig-like creature who'd shown up a few months ago, not to mention her own Biscuit.

"Well, he didn't seem to notice," Lillie said softly, putting down the bottle and grabbing another. "And hopefully, none of them know enough about wine to see that I was lying through my teeth. Shaking it up, honestly. Surprised Karen didn't call me out then and there."

"Probably glad you saved her bacon," Bev said. "I'm not sure she wanted it getting back to Middleburg that her *favorite* wine merchant was selling her bad wine. One might think they did it on purpose."

"Do you think they did?" Lillie asked.

"Who knows?" Bev said. "She's awfully eager to impress Vicky's aunts. I'd thought, at first, she might've killed the flowers to show how well she can handle a crisis, but she certainly was surprised about those bottles. So perhaps…"

"Perhaps someone else is out to get Karen?

Professional sabotage? Oh, the theories practically spin themselves, don't they?" Lillie giggled. "Bev, this really is kind of fun, detangling mysteries and talking to suspects."

"Yes, well, if you decide to be the culprit, do me a favor next time and tell me up front, will you?" Bev scowled at her. "Practically wore a hole in my shoes walking back and forth from Lower Pigsend."

Lillie's smile dampened. "I'm so sorry, Bev. Really, truly. I promise my villain days are over. That's why…" She sighed as she took another bottle. "Honestly, that's why I wanted to fix the wine. Goodness knows, Allen's got enough on his plate. Barely managing to fund all the things Vicky wants to buy for herself. He's been running himself ragged for weeks now. And now, to have to go to Middleburg and argue? Not when I can fix it. I just… I'm so grateful to Allen for this opportunity. I told him what I did in Lower Pigsend—"

"Almost did," Bev said with a look.

"Bev, it was only because Percival showed up that I didn't go through with it," Lillie said, her head hanging. "In any case, I wanted to be up front with him about…about who I was. And you know what he told me? That if *you* thought me trustworthy enough to rent a room to, that was good enough for him." She gave Bev a half-smile. "So I'm doing my best to be as helpful as I can to him. Keep his business running while he's putting out wedding fires, that sort of thing. It's the least I can do for him—and for you."

"The least you can do is *not* get yourself arrested," Bev said. "You don't know these queen's soldiers like I do. I saw Flanigan arrest a man simply for using a ring with a bauble on it." She snapped her fingers and looked back at the inn. "I do hope Allen's told Vicky where he got *her* ring from."

"Where?" Lillie frowned. "It feels…weird, you know? When I get too near it."

"I'm sure it would, to you," Bev said. She explained the barus, and how Allen had gotten the bauble to help with his baking but had never used it. "He had it sized down to a gem he could give Vicky, but I'd hate to find out what Zed would do if he knew what it was."

"Zed seems so nice, though," Lillie said. "And it's his son, and his son's fiancée."

"These soldiers can turn quickly," Bev said. "Some of them can be quite nice, of course, but…" She sighed. "You need to be more careful is all."

"I will. After I deal with this batch of wine, no more magic," Lillie said with a half-smile as she picked up another bottle to cast magic on it.

Bev watched her for a moment, tending to the wine. "What are you doing to it?"

"Oh. Erm. Just tweaking the flavor." She put down the last bottle. "Why?"

"What do you think happened to make it so…

horrible?"

"Hard to say," Lillie said. "I honestly can't tell what part of the process went bad, only that the end product was horrible."

"Do you think it could've been because it sat in the sun too long?" Bev asked.

Lillie considered the wine then shook her head. "It's really hard to say." She eyed Bev. "You don't think Grant did it intentionally, do you?"

"He was the one who retrieved the flower food," Bev said. "But to be honest, I'm really just hoping it's bad luck. I don't want to consider the alternative."

"Well, you know what they say," Lillie replied with a shrug. "If it rains on your wedding day, it's good luck for the marriage."

CHAPTER EIGHT

With the wine crisis averted, everyone went back to their respective homes for a good night's sleep. Bev dreamed fitfully, worrying about Zed asking Lillie too many questions, and Dag Flanigan showing up demanding Bev's head. In the morning, she was groggy and grumpy, but nothing a spot of tea and a helpful nuzzle from Mr. Biscuit didn't fix.

She said a small prayer as she worked her bread dough, hoping that whatever bad luck the couple seemed to have run into would abate. Lillie's comment about rainy days and weddings aside, neither Allen nor Vicky had smiled in weeks, and Bev had to chalk that up to all the added stress.

This morning, Allen brought over the muffins,

looking quite exhausted with large bags under his eyes. He put on a show of a smile for Bev as he placed the goodies on the counter and petted Mr. Biscuit, who greeted him and offered him a supportive nudge to the leg.

"Morning. Sorry, er…sorry about last night," he said, giving the laelaps a good scratch on the butt.

Bev laughed. "What do you mean?"

"Just the argument between me and Vicky and…*him*." Allen glared at the staircase. "Can't believe he hasn't taken the message and left already."

"It would make our room situation easier," Bev said. "I suspect Wallace and Paul will arrive today."

"I hope so. Vicky's starting to fret about *that*, and I thought she couldn't fret about one more thing." He sighed. "I can't wait for this week to be over."

"Chin up, Allen," Bev said, putting her hand on his shoulder. "It's supposed to be a happy occasion, remember?"

"Then why does it seem everything's going wrong?" he asked, almost a little pitifully.

"Oh, come now," Bev said with a laugh. "It's the flowers, which have been fixed, and the wine, which has *also* been fixed." She cleared her throat. "By airing it out, you know."

"Obviously." Allen finally flashed a smile. "Good thing Lillie knows wine, eh?"

"Lillie needs to keep some knowledge to

herself," Bev said. "You remind her of that, okay?"

He nodded. "Vicky wanted me to hang around today and *help*, so I sent Lillie on the cookie deliveries. She's quite the helpful assistant, I have to say. Grateful she's here."

"Your cousin Jacob's been trying to get some time with you," Bev said. "Has he caught up with you yet?"

Allen made a face. "A few times. I know what he's going to talk with me about, and I'm not interested in having that conversation."

Bev waited for him to elaborate, but he didn't.

"Well, I do have a few things to tend to at the bakery. Etheldra's asked for mini pies today, because we don't have enough on our plates, making individual crusts like that." He chuckled, but there wasn't much amusement in it. "Good ol' Etheldra keeping us on our toes. Whatever would we do without her?"

"Live quite boring lives," Bev said with a chuckle.

The first guest down for the day was Karen, who once again wore a severe black outfit that matched her intense personality. She took a muffin, asked Bev if she'd seen Grant (Bev hadn't), then swept through the door, intent on solving the world's problems once more.

Next were Clarice and Jacob, taking the stairs gingerly. The old woman had spent most of the day in her room the day before, but it seemed Jacob wanted her to get some air today. Biscuit's tail wagged, but he respectfully kept his distance as she settled into the chair by the hearth and took a muffin.

"I thought I might take her to the tea shop when it opens," Jacob said.

"Etheldra would be delighted," Bev said.

"Etheldra?" He made a face. "Maybe not, then. She's quite severe, isn't she?"

"I think she'd adore your grandmother," Bev said. Especially since Mr. Biscuit was so keen on Clarice, and Etheldra had a bit of magic of her own. "Etheldra was a big fan of Fernley, you know. They had a great partnership at the tea shop."

"She was such a lovely woman," Jacob said with a sigh as he took a muffin for himself. "Allen's done all right, hasn't he? Taking over for her. Seems that way, as busy as he is."

Bev kicked herself a little for betraying Allen, but Jacob still seemed eager to speak with him. "Allen's sent Lillie on his delivery errands today. I think he's stuck at the bakery making pies this morning, if you'd like to chat with him."

"I've got to tend to Granny this morning," he said. "But I might try to corner him later."

Bev was going to ask more, but Vicky's two aunts appeared. Once again, they wore fine dresses, too fine for Pigsend, but perhaps that was normal for Sheepsburg.

Marion's jewels glimmered in the early morning light, and she carried herself as if she were the queen. "Ah, good morning, John."

"Jacob," he said with a grimace.

"Yes, yes." She took a muffin and sniffed it. "What do we have this morning?"

"Peach muffins," Bev said. "Seems we've finally gotten a good crop of them. If you'd like to visit the farmers' market—"

"Oh, dear." Marion laughed. "Why would I want to visit a dirty market? You're perfectly capable of retrieving the food, are you not?"

Bev gave her a sideways look. "I am, but—"

"These peaches are passable," Marion said. "I'd like a basket of them on the counter here by lunch."

"I'm not..." Bev sighed, adding another item to the long list of favors Vicky owed her. "I'll see what I can do."

"I'd love some peaches," Clarice said from her chair. She'd already devoured her muffin and seemed eager for more. "You know, I have an old family recipe for a peach galette. Supposed to be made with very ripe, sweet peaches, with a sprig of mint for some extra luck. I think it's the thing for this couple."

"Hmph," Marion said, eyeing Clarice as if trying to find fault with her.

"How far is it?" Jacob asked. "Maybe we'll go

there instead of the tea shop."

"Twenty minutes or so," Bev said.

"Zed seems to have disappeared early," Marion said, abruptly changing the subject as if the prior one bored her. "I heard him banging about before dawn."

Bev frowned. "No, I didn't catch him."

"Oh, a man of his stature, I'm sure he's *quite* busy," Marion said with a laugh. "He couldn't *only* be in town for the wedding, after all. Have to search the land for magic."

Bev's lip twitched as she worried about Lillie. But that thought vanished as Karen flew back into the room, gesturing toward the crowd.

"You. Jacob. And Bev. I need you. Come."

There didn't seem much room for argument, and Bev's morning chores were done for the day, so she and Jacob followed, leaving Clarice behind. Karen didn't tell them why they'd been impressed into service, but once they rounded the corner to the town square, the reason became clear. A white fabric tent sat deflated on the ground. From the size of it, it would certainly take up most of the town square, and Bev could see why Vicky had asked Ramone to hold off on reinstalling the dragon fountain.

"Right, we need the lot of you to help get this tent up. It's a multi-person job," Karen said, her voice carrying to the two figures on the other side of the square—Grant, looking put-out to be there, and Dane Sterling. Bev couldn't fathom why the farmer had been pulled off his farm in the southeast to help, as she rarely saw him in town except for town meetings. But perhaps he'd been in the wrong place at the wrong time, and Karen had decided he was necessary for this particular task.

"Yes, now, you," Karen pointed at Grant, "lift this pole. Yes, that's the ticket. Hold it level now, as upright as you can get it. Now you," she pointed at Jacob, "take those ropes and tie them down to the anchors. Yes, that's the way."

"Probably best just to do what she says, eh?" Dane asked Bev as Karen continued barking orders at the pole. "Morning, by the way. Lovely week for a wedding, isn't it?"

"Indeed." She tilted her head. "How'd you get roped into doing this?" She chuckled. "Pun intended."

"Oh, Vicky and Grant's father was my cousin," he said with a nod toward Grant. "I was on my way in to deliver a small present when Ms. Karen asked if I'd help."

"I didn't realize you were related," Bev said, hoping Dane never crossed paths with Vicky's aunts. She'd never seen the farmer take much of an interest in the kids, but there was a lot she didn't see in the town, she supposed.

"Well, Vicky's never been keen on my help, you know. Stubborn to a fault, that one, like her mom. And I've offered Grant a spot at my farm to help out during the harvest, but he's never been interested in that, either." He shrugged. "Try to keep tabs on them as much as I can, but they've got their own lives here in town, and I've got my hands full at the farm."

Bev couldn't help her curiosity. "I've heard some *interesting* stories about Vicky's father. Suppose he had to've been a good man if he'd been better than Griselda's life and money in Sheepsburg."

Dane lifted a shoulder. "There's something to be said for a simple life. Sheepsburg is loud and crowded and full of people with nothing better to do than look down their noses at their neighbor. For all our quirks, the people of Pigsend are a nice bunch, you know?"

Bev had to agree with him there. "Do you know what happened to him?"

Dane shook his head. "He left to fight in the war. After Griselda died, Frank and the kids were struggling. He thought if he won enough battles for the king, he might be able to send some more money back to the kids. But his letters stopped arriving, and no one really knows what happened to him. Never showed up on the rolls, but maybe they weren't so accurate toward the end." He put his hands in his pockets. "I know that's probably part of why Vicky and Grant want nothing to do with me. Probably consider me a reminder of their father. But I knew his heart, and I doubt he'd have abandoned his kids like that."

"Maybe—"

"You!" Karen barked, pointing at Dane. The first pole had been secured, and Allen had been charged to stand next to it. "Come help with this other pole."

The process was repeated at each of the six poles holding the tent aloft on the ends. Then it was time to work on the center pole.

"Okay, you want to align it in there, yes, that's right," Karen said, directing Jacob and Bev, who had the end of the thick pole that would hold the tent up. Grant and Dane were at the other end. "Now, bring that this way."

They picked up the end of the pole and walked it toward the center, as Jacob and Bev lifted their end up until the pole was completely vertical and stuck inside a wooden base.

"There." Karen looked around, eyeing the tent suspiciously. "All right, now we need to adjust the ends again. Bev, you stand here and make sure this doesn't fall down."

Bev stood near the large, wooden pole, keeping her hand on it to feel for any movement as the others flitted around the supporting poles. Once again, the sheer *cost* of this whole endeavor seemed outrageous to her. Between the tent, the town hall, the food, the wine, the inn, the cakes and other sweets…Bev couldn't even begin to guess how much Vicky and Allen had put into this. And all for a single day!

"There." Karen smiled, dusting her hands off. "Now, I've got to head to Middleburg. Don't think I'm going to let the merchant off the hook for sending us that slop disguised as wine." She wrapped her cloak around her shoulders, even though it was quite hot outside.

"Good," Grant said with a huff. "Tired of making that trek anyway."

Karen gave him a sideways look. "Yes. You be sure to stick close to your sister. No telling what she'll need done today. Good to have an extra set of hands nearby."

"I've got to get back to Granny," Jacob said. "Bev, when is that farmers' market supposed to be happening?"

"Oh, now, I suspect," Bev said. "I—"

All conversation ceased when there was a loud *thwap* sound. The center pole began swaying dangerously, which was enough of a warning for the group to dash to safety outside the tent. In slow motion, the center pole fell forward, taking all the others with it. When it stilled, the tent that had taken them over an hour to put up sat in a disheveled heap on the ground.

"What in the..." Bev began, looking at Karen, who was equally dumbfounded.

"I haven't a clue," she murmured, walking toward the tent.

She tossed up the edge, and for a moment, was a figure under the canopy, moving from downed pole to downed pole. She let out a cry of surprise and emerged from the tent with a rope in her hand. Or rather, two pieces of a rope.

"It broke," she said simply. "Took down this pole, and the rest followed."

"Goodness, how did that happen?" Dane asked.

Karen considered the rope for a moment. "The tent isn't the youngest, you know. Lots of weddings have happened under it. Must just...must be at the end of its life." She forced a smile. "Not to worry, I'll...pick up another rope in Middleburg."

"What are we going to tell Vicky?" Grant asked.

Karen hesitated then forced another tight smile that seemed more difficult than the first. "Let's keep this to ourselves, hm? No use in adding to her worries. I'm sure she'll be busy enough with her dress and other things today. If she asks, tell her we aren't scheduled to put it up until later."

Bev nodded, taking the broken rope from her.

"Well, best be off," Karen said with a too-high laugh. "If you'll all pop back by this afternoon, we can give the tent another go, eh? Shouldn't take too long. We've got the hang of it now, don't we?" She seemed to be talking to herself as she pulled on black gloves. "Yes, got the hang of it now. Nothing to worry about."

And with that, she left them standing in the wreckage of the tent.

"That's it!" Grant exclaimed, throwing his arms in the air. "I'm leaving town."

"What? Why?" Bev said.

"It's me, isn't it?" he said, his voice high and strained. "I get the wine, it's sour. I get the flower food, it's wrong. I set up the tent, it falls down." The poor boy looked on the verge of tears, throwing off Dane's comforting hand. "I'm a bad luck charm. Better leave now before the whole wedding ends up ruined."

"You aren't bad luck," Jacob said. "Things happen. Maybe we didn't tie it down well enough."

Bev picked up the frayed rope, inspecting it. She couldn't remember who'd tied this particular one down, but it didn't look to be *cut* or in any way damaged. It did, in fact, look like it had just reached the end of its useful life and had snapped.

Unlucky.

"You can't leave before your sister's wedding," Dane said. "She needs you here—"

"What she needs is a day where nothing goes wrong," he said, turning to Bev. "PJ and his mom are going to visit his grandma in Sheepsburg. I can catch up with them if I hurry."

Bev nodded. Probably for the best that PJ leaves with Zed in town. "Are you sure? What do I tell Vicky?"

"Tell her I'm doing it *for* her," he said, turning to look at the tent. "Because if one more thing goes wrong…" He sniffed. "I don't know what I'll do."

CHAPTER NINE

Bev and Dane had tried to convince Grant to stay, that it was a string of bad luck, but he wouldn't hear of it, making them both promise they'd give Vicky his love and explain why he'd decided to leave. Bev at least got a promise out of him that he'd come back for the ceremony itself, but she wasn't sure how good a promise that it was.

After Bev and Jacob returned to the inn, it didn't take Bev long to get Sin ready. Then she, Jacob, and Clarice were off toward the farmers' market on the warm, late-spring day. Biscuit, too, had whined and pawed at the wagon wheel until Bev put him in the bed with Clarice. He snuggled up next to the old woman, his head on her thigh as she gently stroked his ears.

As they ticked along, Bev watched Jacob. The look of discontent didn't leave his face. He seemed to be scanning the countryside for trouble, and Bev had a hunch it had nothing to do with the tent or Grant.

"So…" Bev began. "That was something about that tent, eh?"

"Probably a sign, to be honest," Jacob said.

"Really? A sign for what?"

"Isn't it obvious? Allen shouldn't marry her," he replied. "She's not right for him."

Bev frowned. "Why do you say that? They seem… Well, they don't seem happy at the moment, but I'm sure that's the stress of the wedding."

"It's more than that," Jacob said. "I'm sure she's lovely. But it seems like they're getting married because it's the thing to do, not because they actually *want* to."

"Because of the baby!" Clarice chimed in.

"Granny," Jacob said with an exasperated sigh. At Bev's quizzical look, his cheeks reddened. "I might've mentioned offhand that I thought Vicky was with child, and that's why they decided to marry. She won't stop mentioning it no matter how often I tell her otherwise."

"You've certainly got a lot of patience with her," Bev said, smiling at the old woman.

"I have to. She's all I have left, other than Allen." He sat back on his hands, some of the tension leaving his face. "I was hoping when I got here that I'd *see* something in Allen that would make me think he wasn't making a huge mistake, but I haven't."

"Oh, well..." Bev adjusted the reins in her hands. "Look, I'm not an expert in love or anything like that. And I won't lie, they've had a bit of a rocky go of it. She's prone to hysterics, and he's prone to secrets. But they seem to have let all that pass now, and they're both eager to tie the knot."

"If you say so." He let out another low sniff.

Bev watched him out of the corner of her eye. Jacob couldn't be the one sabotaging things, could he? "Poor Grant. Can't believe he feels responsible. The tent wasn't his fault. I doubt the wine was, either."

"Strange what happened," Jacob said. "I've never heard of a bottle becoming *better* after it was opened. Normally they go sour, don't they?"

"Lillie knows wine," Bev said lightly. While she didn't think Jacob would talk about magic openly with Zed, she didn't want people to get any more curious than they already were. "Hopefully, Karen will be able to get it all sorted with the vintner. Maybe even get double the wine! I know Vicky's aunts are keen on having it with dinner." She sighed, thinking of this evening. "What do you think we should eat tonight?"

"I do like a good lamb," Clarice said. "What do you think, little laelaps?"

"Dog, Granny. That's a *dog*." Jacob sounded exasperated. "I swear. Half the time I don't know what she's saying."

Bev did. "Say, Clarice," she began, "do you remember life before the war?"

"Sure," she said, lifting her wizened face up to the sky and taking in the warmth of the sun. When she spoke, her voice was clear and measured. "It was a wonderful time. Lots of whimsy and magic in our little town. Creatures like pobyds and centaurs and druids lived next door. Then they all got scared and ran off. Perhaps for the best, as the queen's folk came shortly thereafter, looking for anything with a lick of magic and throwing them in jail."

Bev would've hazarded a guess that a good portion of those creatures now lived below the surface in Lower Pigsend.

"You don't have any magic?" Bev asked.

"Of course she doesn't," Jacob said, a little impatiently.

Biscuit seemed to beg to differ, as his golden eyes watched the old woman like she was a juicy morsel of beef. "I may have a little spark here and there. Somewhere down the line, there might've been a magical person in our history. But nothing worth writing home about, and nothing the queen's folks found particularly interesting." She let out a low chuckle. "They did look!"

"Why do you ask?" Jacob's intense gaze was on Bev.

"I'm always curious," Bev said, explaining her amnesia about events before the war. "Just trying to fill in the puzzle pieces. Life seems much different outside Pigsend."

"Maplewood, the town where we're from, isn't that much different," Jacob said, the tension leaving his face a little. "Quiet, farmland. Lots of folks trying to get by."

Bev nodded, her gaze out on the road beyond. It really was quiet—the sinkholes, Harvest Festival, blackmailers, and dragon shifters aside. And even though the wedding had been adding a frantic slant to things of late, it was a celebration.

As she was mulling things over, she spotted a figure in the middle of a field. At first glance, she thought it was Herman Monday, as it was his farm. But as they drew closer, her brow furrowed.

It was Zed, pointing a three-pronged stick at the ground.

Bev's breath caught in her throat—it was a magical divination rod. She'd used something similar to find the magical river that had been stopped up at the edge of town during the sinkhole debacle. And Karolina Hunter had had a similar one, too.

Back then the soldier had been searching for a powerful object somewhere in town. Bev had been convinced she'd been on the hunt for that mysterious amulet Bev had found in her garden—the one currently residing with a wizard underneath the surface. Was Zed also in town looking for that amulet, or was he searching for something else? Maybe he'd somehow caught wind of Lower Pigsend. The thought was almost too horrible to consider.

The soldier sensed he was being watched. He straightened, spotted Bev and the others on the wagon, and waved, jogging over. By the time he hopped the fence to the road, he wore a wide smile, but Bev couldn't help but notice there was something behind it.

"Well, good morning, you three," Zed said, nodding to Jacob, who glared at him, and Clarice, who surveyed him with mild interest. Biscuit let out a low growl, but with a warning look from Bev, he quieted and rested his head on Clarice's leg again. "What are you doing out and about?"

"Farmers' market," Bev said. "On the hunt for something that will satisfy Marion and Lucy."

"Oh, Lucy's nice enough, isn't she?" Zed said. "But yes, Marion's something of a spitfire. I think I remember hearing as much when Griselda moved to town. But I'm happy to keep her off Allen's plate while he gets things ready for the wedding. She seems to have taken a shine to me, after all."

Based on his affable smile, he was well aware that Marion was only interested in him because of his rank and (presumably) his connections. It was a peculiar smile, one both familiar and strange. Perhaps because Allen never wore one so carefree.

"We're going to get peaches," Clarice said. "Had a taste of those muffins this morning, and simply had to have more. You know, I used to be quite adept in the kitchen. Back before my knees gave me trouble."

"Growing old is tough," Zed said with something of a sympathetic look. "You're Fernley's aunt, aren't you?"

"Indeed I am, you young buck." Clarice leaned over the wagon and smiled at him. "Haven't seen you since you two tied the knot thirty years ago. Wasn't it around here somewhere?"

"At the farm," he said, a little wistfully. "Goodness knows it might be less expensive for Allen to marry somewhere other than the middle of town, but that bride of his has a mind of her own, doesn't she?"

"She's quite a dear," Clarice said. "Too focused on the wrong things, but I'll set her right. Going to make her a peach galette. For luck!"

"Vicky doesn't need you to make her a galette, Granny," Jacob said, a little more forcefully than Bev would've expected. "Allen makes them all day long."

"Yes, but he's never made *my* galette," she said. "The peaches are so juicy right now. I can almost smell them from here."

Zed inhaled. "You must have a better nose than I do. All I can smell is the manure from the farmlands."

Perhaps because he'd been marching around Herman's land. Bev would have to tell the farmer, lest he accuse his sometime nemesis Trent Scrawl of sabotaging his Harvest Festival entry again. "What were you doing on Herman's farm?"

"Oh, out for a stroll. Thought I saw a deer."

Bev was amazed—and a little concerned—at the ease with which he lied. It made her wonder what else he wasn't being truthful about.

Jacob was still glaring at him, as if Zed's very existence was offensive. When he spoke, his tone was dripping with sarcasm. "Have you had a chance to speak with Allen? I'm sure you two have a lot to catch up on."

"Not yet. He's so busy in the bakery. And he's been traveling back and forth all over the country, dropping off pastries and such. Nice to see him having such a ripe ol' business."

"He's at the bakery now," Bev said. "I'm sure you could help him sweep up flour or something like that. Surely, you remember some of what you did with Fernley when you lived in town."

"I may do that." He tapped his fingers to his

forehead. "I suppose I'll see you three at dinner tonight. Have a good trip to the market."

~

Neither Bev nor Jacob felt the need to discuss Zed's strange appearance. Bev didn't want to divulge that she knew about the magical river, and Zed was lying. Jacob, presumably, had his own reasons for the furtive glances he kept throwing toward Zed's retreating back. And Clarice just continued humming to herself, stroking Biscuit's ears and oblivious to the consternation.

Soon after Zed disappeared around the corner, the farmers' market came into view. Jacob helped Clarice get off the wagon, and the woman made a beeline for the stand full of peaches. Bev and Biscuit split away from them, heading over to Alice Estrich's booth. The old farmer was sitting reading a book but brightened when Bev approached.

"Did all those wedding guests eat through everything?" she asked. "Oh, hello there, Biscuit!"

Biscuit had snuck around to the other side of the bench and was sniffing at the tomatoes and carrots stashed back there.

"Biscuit, get back over here," Bev snapped. The laelaps complied, but not before one final sniff at the produce. "Going all right over there?"

"Banner year for produce," she said with a laugh. "Just as soon as I pick the vines, I come out the next day and they're full again. It's a mess." She pulled out a crate and put it on the counter. "What do you think? Feel like taking more off my hands?"

The produce was plump, colorful, and smelled fresh and delicious. Biscuit, too, was back to being interested, climbing up on his hind legs and sniffing intently at the crate. Enough that Bev had to pay attention...especially after running into Zed.

That magical river ran underneath Alice's farm, and if her produce was doing exceptionally well, perhaps that meant it was...Bev wasn't sure. More active? She didn't know if magical rivers crested and waned like regular ones. But it certainly did make for an interesting question.

Could that be causing the trouble for the wedding?

Bev paid Alice a few coins for the produce and loaded it up on the wagon. Jacob and Clarice were talking with Herman Monday, Alice's neighbor. But Bev didn't see Bathilda Wormwood, the farmer who lived on the other side of Alice.

"Hey, Alice," Bev began. "Did Bathilda ever get back from her vacation?"

"Oh, yeah," Alice said. "Few weeks ago."

"Why isn't she here?"

"Retired," Alice said. "Said she managed to save enough money that she could live off that for a while. Talking about selling the farm, too. A little surprise. I knew she was getting up there in age, but I didn't think she'd retire. Not as if I keep track of her expenses, but I can't imagine she was making much as a produce farmer. Most of us get about enough to pay the butcher and maybe a sweet from Allen."

Bev nodded. Bathilda had been able to retire because she'd gotten a herd of magical sheep called tanddaes, which she'd sold to a merchant from Lower Pigsend.

"Glad to know she's made it back," Bev said, after a long pause. "Tell her hello from me, if you see her."

"I'm sure you'll see her at the wedding in a few days," Alice said. "Goodness knows the whole town is invited."

That was certainly true, but Bev would be too busy helping with the food to really get a chance to chat with anyone. She turned and was heading back toward the wagon when she ran into someone who only came up to her stomach.

"Pardon me…oh!"

Staring up at her was a familiar face. Well, not *familiar* per se, but familiar enough. It would be a long time before Bev forgot the particular disdain that Officer Nog sent her way when he looked at her. Of course, the goblin didn't have the usual green tint to his skin, or his elongated teeth. Cloaked in a magical potion, he wasn't the prettiest person, but he certainly wouldn't turn as many heads.

"Watch out, will ya?" he grunted, all but shoving

her out of the way. He had a large sack full of fresh produce, presumably for the citizens of Lower Pigsend. Percival had said he was going to send the goblin on errands for the town, now that they knew they weren't as cut off as they'd thought.

And yet…

"Hello to you too," Bev said, adjusting her shirt. "By the way, you may want to be scarce over the next few days. There's a high-ranking queen's soldier in town. He says he's here for the wedding, but one never knows with them."

Nog gave her a once-over. "You tell him about us?"

"Of course not," Bev said. "And neither has Lillie, for that matter."

He scoffed. "Percival was too nice to her. Letting her off the hook like that. Hope that queen's soldier snaps her up and throws her in jail for what she did."

Bev didn't disagree that Lillie had gotten off lightly, but she couldn't stomach the idea of the pobyd being thrown in jail for no other offense than her own magic. It was about as fair as the Lower Pigsend folks being stuck underground forever.

"Well, I'm just giving you a head's up," Bev said. "Hopefully, after the wedding, he'll have moved on. But until then…" She paused. "Does Percival know anything about the magical river? Seems to be making the crops a little—"

"If you got a question for Percival, go ask him yourself," Nog snapped, hoisting the bag onto his back. "I gotta get back before Shamus gives me an earful."

That, or he was eager to tell the wizard apprentice about the queen's soldier in town.

Bev let him go, chewing her lip. She hoped the goblin would take her warning to heart and stay underground for at least the next few days. But one never knew with Officer Nog.

Chapter Ten

The trio returned to the inn, Bev's wagon laden with three baskets of peaches, bright red strawberries, beautifully plump blueberries, not to mention tomatoes, potatoes, carrots, and peas. Clarice held the basket of peaches she'd gotten for her tarts in her arms like it was precious gold, and Jacob kept scowling at the world as if it had personally offended him. When they arrived back at the inn, Jacob helped his granny and the produce off the wagon then stared at the bakery with a sigh.

"Suppose I'd better stop mucking around and go talk with him," he said. "Granny, will you be all right here at the inn by yourself?"

"Oh, yes. Gotta get going on this galette." She

turned to Bev. "If that's all right with you."

"Absolutely," Bev said with a smile. "Come on, I'll get you set up."

Bev found Clarice a stool and set it by the kitchen table, along with a small paring knife and bowl, and Clarice carefully and thinly sliced the peaches.

"Now, the crust." She patted the table. "I'll need some flour, sugar, salt, butter, an egg, and a bit of milk."

Bev found the ingredients, placing them on the table next to Clarice as she finished slicing the peaches. She measured the flour into a bowl then added a small palmful of sugar and a pinch of salt. After that, she took the butter Bev had gotten from her root cellar and began working it into the mixture.

"Got to really work it in there," Clarice said. "And be quick, else the butter will melt."

"You seem to be quite adept at baking," Bev said, having seen a similar sort of recipe in Fernley's stash of cards. "Is it a family trait?"

"If you're asking if I'm a pobyd, like that gal across the street, I'm afraid not." She chuckled. "Though with our family's penchant for all things baking, it's probably not too far off the mark to think we had one somewhere along the line."

Bev started. "You know Lillie's a—" She glanced at the closed door to the front room. "Maybe let's keep that to ourselves."

"Oh, fine, fine. That soldier being around, I can understand why you're so antsy about it." Clarice seemed unbothered by the idea, as she added some milk and the single egg, using her hands to mix the dough together.

"Do Allen or Jacob have any magic?" Bev asked. She'd always wondered about Allen, if he'd somehow come into his magic or if he was born without it.

"No. His mother was the last of it, like Jacob's mother was the last of hers." She sighed. "Such a wonderful group we were before the war. I had a cousin who was the chef for the king! Once upon a time..." She tutted. "But suppose it's for the best the boys don't have any magic to speak of. Jacob spends half his time shooing queen's soldiers away from my door, though they found me wanting the times they've tested me for magic."

"Tested you?" Bev asked. "How?"

"Different ways," she said. "But I think they knew the moment I agreed to their test that there was nothing of interest. Her Majesty likes creatures with the full range of abilities, not the hints I carry." She smiled. "I do have a few tricks up my sleeve. This galette, in particular, is an old family recipe. Peaches, for longevity and health. Apricots for prosperity and longevity. Mint, for luck—which they could certainly use. And a bit of honey for truth and knowledge." She paused, counting her fingers. "Yes, that's the lot of it."

"Are those magical ingredients?" Bev asked.

"Depends on the practitioner," she said with a laugh. "In the hands of your friend Lillie, they might be. But in mine, it's more like a recipe for good intentions."

Bev looked at her sideways. "Does Jacob seem… unhappy with the wedding?"

"Oh, yes. Poor thing. He's quite upset about losing Allen."

"Losing Allen?" Bev chuckled. "That's a bit extreme, isn't it? He's getting married. It's not like he's dying."

Clarice floured the table and turned the dough out onto it. "Before Fernley died, the two boys were thick as thieves. Allen was always coming to spend a week with us, or Jacob here to visit Allen. But when Allen started taking the bakery a bit more seriously, he stopped coming to visit every month. Now, it'll be even less. Poor Jacob doesn't have any other friends. Hard to make them when you've got to spend all your time with your granny, you know?" She sighed. "I wished for a different life for him. He wasn't supposed to be the one to stay and take care of me. But everyone else is gone."

"Do you think…" Bev began quietly. "Jacob wouldn't do anything to ruin the wedding, would he?"

"Well, he'd like Allen not to marry the girl," she said with a chuckle. "But I think at the end of the day, if Allen's happy, Jacob will be happy, too." She paused. "The problem is he doesn't think Allen is happy. That's why he's trying to convince him to call off the wedding."

"How far would he go to convince him of that?"

"I'm sure a good talking to," Clarice said. "Do you have a rolling pin?"

Bev handed it over. "I'm worried someone's behind all these mishaps. That they're hoping enough will go wrong that Vicky and Allen will call it off. Jacob said he thought the tent going down was a sign."

Clarice rolled the dough into a circle, humming to herself and not answering. Bev waited, watching her closely, but Clarice finished rolling out the dough.

"What about that mint and apricot jam? Maybe some honey, too, if you can spare it."

"I'll have to pop over to Etheldra's for the mint, and I'm sure Allen has some jam on hand," Bev said. "Give me about half an hour."

"Then let's put this dough somewhere cool so it doesn't melt," Clarice said. "And I'll be happy to sit in the front room."

Bev did as instructed, first setting Clarice in the chair then taking her dough to the root cellar. But before she could walk out the door, a short, businesslike man walked through it, carrying a suitcase in one hand and a briefcase in another. Without as much as a "hello," he marched up to the front desk and put down his bags.

"Good morning," he said, adjusting his glasses. "Are you the proprietor of this establishment?"

Bev let out a smile. "Erm. Yes."

"My name is Duckett Morley." He bowed, slightly. "This is Pigsend, is it not?"

"It is." Bev nodded. "What can I do for you, Mr. Morley?"

He puffed out his chest as he inspected a small piece of paper. "I'm here to witness the wedding of Ms. Victoria Hamblin to," he looked at his paper, "Mr. Allen Mackey."

"Oh, you are," Bev said. "You're a bit early for that. It's not for another three days."

He didn't seem deterred. "Well, then I require a room at the inn until such time that the wedding occurs."

"I'm so sorry," Bev said, and was genuinely so. Mr. Morley looked like he'd traveled quite a ways to get to town. "Unfortunately, we're all booked up at the inn until after the wedding."

He let out a sigh. "Well, suppose that's as well. Can you point me to the location of the other inns in town so I may inquire there?"

"I'm the only one," Bev said with a small wince. "I hope you didn't travel far. I do apologize for the inconvenience. There should be more availability in Middleburg. It's up the road."

He let out a harrumph. "I suppose I'll head back to Middleburg. When, exactly, is this wedding supposed to take place again?"

"Three days from now," Bev said. "At four o'clock in the afternoon."

"Then I shall see you in three days' time. Good day."

By the time Bev walked outside, Mr. Morley was gone. He seemed such a strange individual and had given no other information about why he needed to witness the wedding, but perhaps all that was for the best. The last thing Vicky and Allen needed was another interloper requiring the shuffling of rooms. While she was starting to worry about the cleric, she was somewhat grateful his absence meant her difficult discussion with Marion and the rest would be put off a little while longer.

Speaking of Vicky's aunts, Bev spotted them sitting in the window table at Etheldra's, along with Nadia, who Bev hadn't really spoken to yet. The three sipped their tea out of delicate teacups, finer than Bev had seen Etheldra dole out to her usual customers. But Marion's attitude required a bit more refinement, even from Etheldra.

"Morning, Bev," Shasta Brewer said from behind the counter. Etheldra was nowhere to be seen.

"What can I do for you today?"

"Need to pick up a bit of mint. Fresh, if you've got it," Bev said. "But I suppose dried would be all right, too."

Shasta brightened. "I've got a pot growing out in the back. Well, Etheldra does. Come on. Let's cut you off a few sprigs." She paused, leaning over. "Erm. Mrs. Bilensbrook? Ms. Edelbert? Do you mind if I pop out back for a moment to help Bev?"

"Yes, we should be—" Lucy began.

"I'd be putting on another kettle, Shasta. Never know when your customers want a fresh cup of tea, do you?"

Shasta's face twitched, but she filled the kettle with water from the pitcher and put it on the small stove. Then she gestured silently to Bev, who followed her through the back room, filled with tea tins and smelling faintly of tea and herbs, to the back courtyard. There, Bev found Earl and Etheldra with a teacup each.

"Are they gone yet?" Etheldra barked at Shasta.

"Not yet, ma'am," Shasta said.

The owner harrumphed and picked up her cup. "Wonder if they're planning to sit here all morning and drink my tea? Scaring off all my customers. I have lots to do in there, you know."

Bev hid a smile. Seemed even Etheldra could only take so much of Marion.

"Well, here you go," Shasta said, handing Bev a

few sprigs from the mint plant in the corner. "Is this enough?

"Should be fine." Bev cleared her throat. "So did you and Stella get the maid of honor thing sorted?"

Shasta's face fell. "Yes, in fact. Marion told us both we had no business even thinking we'd be her maids of honor. Nadia is now on the hook for all of it."

"Speech included?" Bev asked with a laugh. She'd barely heard the girl utter three words.

Shasta lifted a shoulder. "Apparently, speeches are uncouth. But Marion *assures* us that she will be happy to say a few words, since Vicky's parents aren't here to do it."

"I'm sure Vicky is…very happy to have her aunt here," Bev said, albeit with much difficulty. "She's certainly…taken charge of things."

"If that's what we're calling it," Etheldra barked. "Can't wait for this whole bloody affair to be over and done with. She's scaring off all my usual customers, and she insists on coming every day and sitting right there."

And you're making poor Shasta take care of her, too. "I'm sure she's not—"

"*Shasta! That kettle is whistling!*" Marion's voice echoed from inside.

"Well, better go tend to that," Shasta said. "Let me know if you need more mint." She dashed inside.

"What did you need mint for, Bev?" Earl asked.

"Allen's aunt Clarice is making him and Vicky a peach galette," Bev said with a smile. "She wanted to add some mint for luck."

Etheldra took an ominous sip of her tea. "They're going to need more than mint, mark my words."

Bev didn't stick around to find out what Etheldra was thinking, or to speak with Vicky's aunts, as she had one more stop to make before returning to the inn. Allen would have honey, and with as much fruit as Bev had seen Lillie carting back from the farmers' market, he was sure to have jam. Whether he'd have apricot jam specifically was another story, but it never hurt to ask.

When she walked into the bakery, raised voices stopped her in her tracks.

"You're being pigheaded!" Jacob barked. "You can't see that you're absolutely miserable."

"Maybe I'm miserable because my best friend is telling me I shouldn't get married!" Allen yelled back, sounding angrier than Bev had ever heard him. "You've been trying to ruin our relationship since we got together—"

"Which time?" Jacob cried. "Because you two have been on and off since you got together. How long is this on gonna last before she overreacts to something, or you snap over something ridiculous?"

"When that happens, it won't be your problem, now will it?"

"You're right. Because I'm going back to Maplewood."

"W-what?" Allen sounded genuinely shocked. "You can't *leave*. You're my best man!"

"I can't, in good conscience, stand there and watch you make a giant mistake. So I'm leaving."

"Allen?" Bev called, putting the mint down on the counter and walking around to the back room. "Is everything all right?"

Jacob was visible for a moment before slamming the back door behind him. Allen, wearing a coating of flour, stared at the door for a long moment before shaking his head and returning to the large bowl of cookie dough.

"What was *that* about?" Bev said, when Allen didn't speak.

"Jacob was letting me know his feelings about my wedding," Allen replied, his voice dull and lifeless. "I told him if he didn't want to watch it, then he could go back home." He lifted his gaze to look out the window. "Suppose that's where he's going now."

"Oh, Allen, it was a row. He won't leave before the wedding," Bev said. "Here, Clarice has sent me to fetch some apricot jam and honey from you. She's making you and Vicky a peach galette that's supposed to be for good luck."

"Don't have any jams," Allen said. "Honey, right over there in that jar."

"No...jams?" Bev frowned. "I've seen Lillie coming from the farmers' market practically every day."

"No idea what she's doing with them, but I haven't had a chance to make a jam in weeks. Probably going to regret it come winter, but..." He dug his fingers into the dough and worked it. "Suppose that's a problem I can deal with then. We can have a season of breakfast biscuits."

Bev sighed, walking over to Allen. "Are you all right?"

"Not really," Allen said, stopping. "What he said... Bev, what if he's right? What if I'm making a mistake? I love Vicky, but..."

Bev didn't know what to say. "I think only you can make that call. The rest of us are onlookers, you know? But Clarice tells me Jacob's a bit jealous of your time. Feels like you're abandoning him. That's probably why he's acting the way he is."

"That's dumb," Allen said.

"Well, people can act funny when faced with a big life change," Bev said. "I'm sure he'll be back at the inn this evening, ready to apologize and put everything behind you."

CHAPTER ELEVEN

Jacob wasn't at the inn that night. Nor was Grant, for that matter. Bev had the unfortunate job of telling Vicky that her brother had skipped town, which was met by a snort of derision from Allen. It seemed Jacob wasn't the only one who assumed Grant had left to shirk responsibility.

Dinner was, blessedly, a low-key affair. Wallace and Paul hadn't shown up, so Bev could push off the room conversation another night. Karen hadn't returned from Middleburg, but her presence was barely missed as Marion dominated the conversation. Etheldra, to her credit, kept her mouth shut, but glowered at the other woman nearly the entire time she was downstairs. Vicky and

Allen sat alone at one of the tables, having whispered arguments with one another that ended in dirty stares.

"What in the world are you two arguing about?" Marion finally asked, midway through the meal.

"It appears Allen's best man has left without a word," Vicky said. "And he won't tell me why."

Allen cleared his throat, annoyed. "We had a difference of opinion, and it seems it was too great to overcome. He decided he wasn't going to stick around."

"What a racket," Vicky said, tutting at him. "What could be so awful that he couldn't stand to watch you get married?"

Allen's cheeks went pink, and Bev knew he was trying hard not to hang Vicky out to dry, especially in front of her aunts. "It's not important."

"I think it is," Vicky said, clearly not getting the hint.

"It's not."

"Obviously, it is, if he thinks—"

"I think the boys got a bit too hot under the collar," Bev broke in. "Probably a big misunderstanding. I'm sure Jacob will be back tomorrow."

That seemed to satisfy Marion, but not Vicky, who continued to scowl at her fiancé. Allen, to his credit, kept his attention on his food and didn't engage.

Once Marion had retired, the rest of the diners excused themselves one by one, until the affianced couple and Zed picked at their plates in silence, and Clarice snoozed in a chair near the fire.

Zed, who'd kept to himself most of the evening, smiled tentatively and turned toward the couple. "So, Allen—"

"I've got to get back to the bakery," Allen muttered, pushing his half-eaten dinner away. "Long night."

"Oh! Before you go." Clarice awoke as if someone had pinched her. "I have a gift."

"You didn't need to get us anything," Vicky said, her plastered-on smile not quite as bright as it had been.

Allen seemed torn but love for his great-aunt won out and he sat back down.

"Let me go get it," Clarice said, shakily getting to her feet.

"You sit," Bev said, going to the old woman and helping her sit next to the couple. "I'll get it."

Bev dashed into the kitchen to get the peach pastry off the table, hissing at Biscuit who was up on his hind legs, sniffing intently. Luckily, she'd had the foresight to put it far out of reach of his darting tongue.

She brought it out, earning half-hearted coos from the couple, and a proud clap from the old woman.

"Now, listen closely, because this was made intentionally," Clarice said, before naming each ingredient and its purpose.

Bev kept an eye on Zed, who seemed to consider the old woman amusing and not dangerous. But she still wasn't sure what he'd been doing in Herman's farmland earlier that day, so she didn't trust him.

"Now," Clarice clapped her hands, "you'll need to eat a large piece of it, of course, to get the full effect."

"Oh, I'm not really that hungry—" Vicky began but Clarice wouldn't hear of it, pushing the plate closer to her.

Allen took a bite, as did Vicky, and their eyes lit up almost in unison. "This is amazing," Allen said. "Tastes like my mom's recipe."

"She probably stole it from us," Clarice said with an affectionate smile. "Most of her best work came from our side of the family, you know. You'll be making those wedding cookies, right?"

He nodded.

"Many a long marriage has been started by those cookies," Clarice said.

"We had those cookies at our wedding, too," Zed said.

Allen's smile was gone in an instant, and he glared at his father.

Clarice was undeterred. "Eat up, Allen. Don't you dare leave a crumb behind. Goodness knows you need a change in luck, and this is the thing to do it."

Bev awoke the next morning, feeling more confident about the day. She took care cleaning and doing her chores, hoping the good intentions would help the luck found in that pastry. But if she were being honest...the luck might change because the person ruining the wedding had skipped town. If nothing else happened between now and the wedding, Bev would know for sure it was Jacob.

Lillie arrived with a basket of raspberry muffins, which she placed next to Bev with a smile. "Morning, Bev."

"Morning, Lillie," Bev said. "Listen...I stopped by the bakery yesterday looking for some jam."

"Oh, I think we're fresh out," she said, tapping her chin. "Should probably make some—"

"That's the thing," Bev said. "What have you been doing with all that fruit you've been buying at the farmers' market?"

Lillie's cheeks went pink. "Well, have to be getting back to the bakery. See you later, Bev." She scampered through the door before Bev could say another word.

Curious. Then again, perhaps Lillie was eating all the fruit, as she'd been deprived of it these past five years. It wasn't very surprising, thinking about it like that. Bev shook her head and decided to leave it be.

The inn was bustling shortly after that, and Bev was content to sit in the front room and listen to the conversations. Karen had come back sometime late in the night and had rushed out the door without grabbing a muffin. Zed, too, had skipped out early without speaking with anyone. Left were Marion and Nadia, discussing their plans for the day (or rather, Marion was dictating, and Nadia was nodding silently), and Lucy had helped Clarice down the stairs, and was chatting with her about Jacob's sudden disappearance.

"He'll be back," she said to Lucy's concern. "They ate that whole galette yesterday, didn't they?"

"Well, good," Marion said. "Vicky will need her strength today."

"What's on the agenda?" Bev asked.

"Final dress fittings," Lucy said with a content smile. "I can't wait to see what sort of dress Vicky's designed for herself."

"I have my doubts about her taste, but I hope it'll be passable," Marion said. "And Nadia, of course. She's much taller than those Brewer twins. It may take all day to get the maid-of-honor dress tailored to her size."

Karen arrived, full of fury and purpose, but softened and brightened when her gaze landed on Vicky's aunts.

"Apolinary is ready for you," she said, opening

the door with a flourish. "Come, come, Vicky's already getting into her dress."

"Oh, exciting," Lucy said.

As soon as they were through the door, Karen's sharp gaze went to Bev. "You. I need you to get Vicky's bouquet from my room."

Bev looked around, confused. "Can't you do it?"

"Obviously, I've got to escort Mrs. Bilensbrook and Ms. Edelbert to the seamstress shop. Then I've got to get this blasted tent set up."

And with that, the door shut.

"Vicky, you sure owe me," Bev muttered, turning to walk up the stairs.

As a rule, Bev didn't intrude on her guests' privacy, so it was a bit strange to see her room filled with various black tunics and dramatic capes. But against the wall, five bouquets sat in vases on the floor, bathed in sunlight. Bev picked up the largest one, vase included, and, with the utmost care, cradled it as she descended the stairs and headed to the seamstress shop.

It wasn't too far, but Bev didn't want to think of what Vicky might say if anything happened to her bouquet. Bev opened the front door to the seamstress shop, which was once again aflutter with conversations and arguments. Vicky stood in the center of the room wearing a long, beautiful white dress that didn't seem finished (or as finished as Bev would've expected this close to the wedding). At her feet, Apolinary was kneeling, fiddling with the hem. And next to Apolinary was Rosie Kelooke, the retired seamstress who owned a flock of demonic chickens. Vicky's aunts hadn't arrived yet; Karen had taken them the long way, she supposed.

"If you put the hem there," Rosie snapped at Apolinary, "it will be too short when you add all the petticoats."

"We aren't adding that many petticoats," Apolinary retorted, sounding like this conversation had been going on too long.

"Well, you *should*. It is a wedding, after all."

Vicky caught Bev's reflection and exhaled. "Bev, bring that bouquet here so we can check the colors. I think we need to dye the lace a darker color—"

"It's your wedding day," Apolinary said. "If we dye the lace any darker, it'll look brown. You don't want your wedding dress to be brown, do you?"

"No, but it needs to *pop*," Vicky said, taking the bouquet from Bev. She held it between her hands and squared her shoulders, staring at her reflection as if it would reveal the secrets of the world. After a moment, she handed the bouquet back to Bev. "Just a *hint* darker—"

"Vicky, if you want to dye the lace, we'll have to undo all of it," Apolinary said, patiently. "Then dye it then let it dry. Then reapply it to the dress."

"Yes, I know."

"When are we going to have time to accomplish that?" Apolinary asked, gesturing to the three other dresses on dress forms against the wall. They, like the wedding dress, were half-finished, perhaps also due to Vicky's inability to make a decision. "The Brewer twins will be here any minute, as will your aunts—"

"Already here." Marion stepped over the threshold, looking too big for the small seamstress shop. Beside her, Lucy wore a softer smile, and Nadia looked bored, as usual. Karen didn't follow, as she was already headed toward the town square, her pace quick. "If you aren't early, you're late. Isn't that what Papa used to say, Lucille?"

"It is." The other sister nodded. "Vicky, you're a vision. What a lovely dress."

Vicky's face lit up in relief. "Do you think so? Really?"

Before Lucy could respond, Marion strode forward to inspect the dress. "Well, I must say, it's quite simple for a wedding, but I suppose sometimes simple can be effective. The lace, though, it's a bit dark, isn't it? Perhaps you should scrap it and try something a bit whiter, hm?" She gestured to the hem. "And surely, you aren't going to wear so few petticoats? You need something with some volume. It's your wedding day, after all."

She continued critiquing the dress, highlighting everything Vicky had, and then some. Apolinary seemed to be growing more agitated by the moment, but Rosie smiled and nodded approvingly.

"You are a woman of exquisite tastes," Rosie said, extending her hand. "Rosie Kelooke. I was the seamstress in town before my hands gave out, and I sold the business to Apolinary here."

"Charmed, I'm sure," Marion said, giving the other woman's outfit an appraising look. Based on the quirk of her lips, Rosie passed muster. "Now, back to this mess of a wedding gown." Marion lifted the skirt weakly and let it fall. "No, no, this is all wrong. I can tell what you're going for, dear Victoria, but you really should start all over."

"We don't have *time* to start over," Apolinary said through gritted teeth. "I've got three other dresses to finish, not to mention the other workload of our regular customers."

"Victoria's wedding takes priority, doesn't it?" Marion asked. "She does *work* for you, doesn't she?"

"Yes, but—"

"Then I don't see why it's a question." Marion swept to the gowns by the wall. "I can only assume these half-finished pieces are the bridesmaids' gowns." She shook her head. "Goodness me, they're identical!"

"Yes, bridesmaid dresses usually are," Apolinary said, bending down to stab the hem of the dress with perhaps more force than was necessary.

"Victoria, which is Nadia's dress?" Marion asked, gesturing to the set. "Your maid of honor should stand apart from the others."

Vicky's cheeks colored. "I haven't quite decided who's going to be the maid of honor, as I told you. I have two very dear friends in town, and—"

"Nonsense. Your cousin Nadia will be your maid of honor. She's family, after all. About the only one you've got left, besides your Aunt Lucy and myself." She tittered. "I don't think you want us standing up there with you!"

"No, but—"

"Nadia, why don't you try this one?" Marion said, pushing one dress form toward her daughter. "We'll have to figure out the best way to make it *pop* as the maid of honor. Maybe a splash of pink or a vibrant blue. Something to really catch the eye of the crowd."

"Isn't the eye of the crowd supposed to be on Vicky?" Bev offered lightly.

Marion turned to Bev in the corner, her lip curling. "Shouldn't you be back at the inn tending to things?"

"Things are tended," Bev replied with a bright smile. "Karen asked me to bring Vicky's bouquet. To check the color, right?"

"Right." Vicky turned to the mirror again. "So you think it's too dark—"

"I think it's *fine*," Apolinary cut in before Marion could go off on another tangent. "I think we're three days from your wedding, and we don't have time to be overturning the apple cart. Nobody's going to remember what the dress looked like, but they will remember if it's half-finished."

"I beg to differ," Rosie interjected. "Every bride who's worn one of *my* dresses was spoken about for months afterward." She turned to Marion. "I had several write-ups in the Middleburg newspapers, you know. I was quite the in-demand seamstress."

"*Was*," Apolinary said. "Rosie, thank you so much for your time, but—"

"If you're *so stretched* for time," Marion said. "Why don't you work on Nadia's dress, Rosie? You're the experienced seamstress, after all."

Rosie rubbed her hands, as if her arthritis were already acting up at the thought of it. "Well, only if Apolinary thinks she can't handle it."

"I think if you want to help with Nadia's dress, that would be lovely." Unsaid but plain on Apolinary's face: *If it means I rid myself of the two of you, all the better.*

"Then that's settled." Rosie turned to Marion and Nadia with a bright smile. "Come, Nadia, why don't you try it on, and we'll see what we can do with it."

She shuffled the two toward the small changing room, leaving Vicky with Apolinary, Lucy, and Bev. Vicky sighed as she poked at her dress, her face drooping.

"Do you really think it's too plain, Aunt Lucy?"

she whispered.

"I think…" Lucy sighed. "I think you could add a few things here and there. It might be a little simple, but nothing this seamstress can't fix up for you." She tilted her head. "Don't you mind Marion. You know she's got plenty of opinions."

"More than I'd like to hear, that's for sure." Apolinary stood. "Well, Vicky? What are we doing? Scrapping the whole thing or working with what we have?"

While they dithered back and forth, Bev started inching toward the exit, as she had nothing to add. But before she could move more than a single step, something acrid hit her nose. She inhaled, the scent becoming clear.

"Do you smell smoke?" Bev asked, sniffing the air.

"I—" Vicky's eyes widened then she let out a scream.

The hem of her dress was on fire.

CHAPTER TWELVE

At once, every person in the shop sprang into action. Vicky spun wildly. Apolinary chased after her to step on the flame. Marion and Lucy ran over, the latter with her hands over her mouth, the former crying out in panic as she told someone to fetch water. Rosie sprinted around the shop, yelling something about how she *always* had spare water in case something went alight.

And Bev, realizing the bouquet she'd brought held a sizable quantity of water, yanked the bouquet out of the vase and tossed the water onto the small flame to douse it. Thankfully, it was enough, but in the few minutes the fire had spread, it had eaten a large hole in the back of Vicky's dress.

For a moment, no one could speak. Then Vicky's face turned beet red as she waved her hands frantically in front of her face, breathing heavily and with some difficulty.

"Steady on, Vicky," Bev said, placing a bracing hand at Vicky's back. "Deep breaths. You're okay. Everything is fine. Fire is out."

"But my *dress!*" Vicky exclaimed, tears bursting from her eyes. "It's ruined!"

"It's nothing we can't fix," Apolinary said, stooping to inspect the damage. Her face was hidden from Vicky, but Bev could read the worry as plain as day as she thumbed the singed fabric. "Yes, we can fix this. It's fine."

Vicky sobbed openly into her hands.

"How did it happen?" Bev asked, walking around to where Vicky had been standing. There was nothing except a patch of sunlight that seemed awfully hot. Bev followed the beam to the window, where a water glass was perched on the sill.

Bad luck, indeed.

Bev moved the glass, and the beam of light seemed less intense. "I think I've found the culprit. Looks like the sun was coming through this glass at the wrong angle."

Apolinary walked over to inspect the glass, putting it in the window again and moving it away, watching the light as Bev had. "That's..."

"It's *bad form*," Rosie said. "Putting a glass in

the window like that. When *I* ran the shop—"

"You didn't ever put a glass in the window?" Bev asked with a quirked brow.

Rosie sniffed. "Well, I never had anything of mine catch on fire."

Vicky sniffled, her shoulders shaking as she wiped away tears. "W-what are w-we g-going to d-do?"

"I'm going to fix this," Apolinary said with a firm nod. "It'll be perfect by your wedding day."

"Everybody's going to fix everything," Vicky said, taking the handkerchief Lucy offered. "Why isn't anything going right to begin with?"

Nobody seemed to have an answer.

"Why don't we get you out of this dress so Apolinary can start working on it?" Bev said, gesturing to the dressing rooms. "I'm sure we can get you something warm and calming at Etheldra's."

"I think we could *all* use something calming," Marion said with a dramatic hand to her chest as Vicky sniffled her way to get changed. "But that tea shop, I haven't found anything there I like yet—"

"Then why don't you come to my home?" Rosie said. "I've got plenty of space, and we can continue work on Ms. Nadia's dress?"

"Yes, great idea," Apolinary muttered, walking to a large bolt of fabric and measuring with her arm.

"I think I'll stay behind and tend to Vicky," Lucy said, casting a long look at the dressing room.

"Suit yourself," Marion said. "Come, Rosie, to your house."

The room seemed much quieter with Marion and Rosie gone. Lucy slipped into the dressing room, appearing only for a moment to hand Apolinary the ruined dress before returning to help Vicky.

"What a mess," Apolinary said with a heavy sigh as she inspected the damage again. "And I'd thought the day couldn't get any worse when Rosie walked in."

"What's *that* about?" Bev asked, keeping her voice low. "Rosie's been retired for a few years now, hasn't she?"

"Supposedly," Apolinary said with a dirty look. "She's never felt like I run the business as well as she did. Likes to give us large dress orders to make sure I know what I'm doing, then bring them back for tons of alterations because they aren't *right*." She sighed, looking at the damaged dress. "I wouldn't put it past her to have placed that glass in the window to make my job harder."

Bev chewed her lip. "It was an accident."

"So you say," Apolinary said. "But if it was an accident, it was well-targeted. I've got to redo the *entire* skirt. All the lace will have to be redone, too. I'm going to have to ask Rosie to do the Brewer twins' dresses too, at this rate. Though I hope Aunt Marion drives her as mad as she does me."

She smiled evilly, but it was gone as soon as Vicky emerged with her aunt. She was pale, her eyes red, and her bottom lip trembled as Lucy sat her on a chair to steady herself.

"Everything's going wrong." Vicky sniffed, tears streaming down her face.

"Oh, not *everything*," Bev said. "You're still getting married, aren't you?"

Vicky turned to her. "Has Wallace arrived yet?"

"Well, no," Bev said with a wince. "Not that I'm aware."

"We can't get married without the cleric!" Vicky said with a cry, much to the chagrin of Lucy and Apolinary. "Maybe they fell into a ditch or something? Maybe they decided they didn't want to come?"

"I'm sure they've just been waylaid," Bev said gently. "And who knows, they may be at the inn waiting right now? Let's get you over to Etheldra's for a spot of tea, and I'll head right back to there to check, hm?"

～

Vicky was still a bit unsteady on her feet, so Bev and Lucy half-carried her to the tea shop, which was thankfully empty, save Shasta behind the counter. The twin took one look at her friend, dropped the tea bag she was filling, and rushed over, kneeling beside her.

"Vicky, darling, what happened?" she said,

taking Vicky's hand. "Has Allen called things off?"

Vicky looked at her as if she'd told her Allen had died. *"What?"*

"Everything's fine," Bev said with a sideways look at Shasta. "We had a small mishap with Vicky's dress. She's a little upset about it. Do you have any calming teas you could brew her?"

Shasta nodded and headed back to the large wall of tea tins, picking something off the wall and putting on the kettle. Etheldra appeared from the back room and scanned the shop until her gaze landed on Vicky. She let out a low *harrumph* and walked over.

"What in the world is wrong with you, girl?" Etheldra barked.

"Vicky's dress caught on fire," Bev said. "It's fine, she's fine, but—"

"She's clearly not *fine*. Look at her," Etheldra said, picking up Vicky's chin to look her in the eye. "Right. Shasta, whatever you've got, throw it away. Vicky needs something more potent."

Shasta gave her boss a confused glance then put the tea back in the tin and frowned. "What—"

"Never you mind, girl." Etheldra walked into the back room, then reappeared back with a bag in her hand and set to the tea kettle, which was still warming up. She pulled a small vial from beneath her dress and poured it in the cup.

"What's that?" Vicky asked, sniffing.

"Whiskey," Etheldra said.

Bev put her hand on Vicky's shoulder and squeezed. "Can I leave her with you three? I want to check on Apolinary then head back to the inn."

Shasta nodded, sitting across from Vicky and taking her hand. "We've got her, Bev."

"Go on back to whatever you're doing," Etheldra said, walking over with a teacup that smelled *very strongly* of whiskey and not much else. "Vicky's in good hands here. Drink this. All of it— every drop. When you're done, I'll make you another one."

"Do you have any more?" Lucy said, a little weakly. "My heart is still aflutter."

Etheldra surveyed her. "Fine. Bev. Come with me to get it."

Bev gave her a sideways look but followed the tea shop owner to the back room anyway.

"So," Etheldra said, fiddling with a tin on a shelf, "what's going on with our dear Vicky? Her *dress* caught on fire?"

Bev sighed, telling Etheldra about the freak accident. "Just a spot of bad luck, that's all. When it rains, it pours," Bev replied. "Nothing too bad, though. Everything is fixable. Apolinary says it's not..." Bev couldn't really tell Etheldra that. "Well, Apolinary might not sleep until the wedding day, but it'll get done."

"Mm-hm." Etheldra turned to her.

Bev frowned. It wasn't like her to hold back her opinion. "Why? What do *you* think is going on?"

"Well, to me, it sounds like Vicky's been cursed."

Bev let out a barking laugh. "Cursed? What in the world...? Who could possibly want to *curse* Vicky?"

Etheldra shrugged. "No one person can possibly attract this much trouble in such a short amount of time. The sour wine, the wrong flower food, now her dress catching on fire because it was close to a *window*?" Etheldra put her hands on her hips. "Once is bad luck, twice is something to talk about, thrice is something worth investigating. I *assume* you are investigating."

"Why would you..." That was a dumb question. "How am I supposed to investigate a cursed girl?"

"Clearly, you find the person who cursed her," Etheldra said, putting the tin away. "So who's got it out for Vicky? Or Allen?"

"Well, I'd thought Grant or Jacob, but both of them have left town, so—"

"What does that have to do with anything?" Etheldra said. "They could've cast the curse, and—"

"Or it's something else entirely," Bev said, holding up her hands. "Hendry's convinced it's the wedding planner causing problems intentionally to make herself look like a better crisis manager."

"I could certainly see that," Etheldra said.

"Except it doesn't explain how a dress could catch fire. Unless, of course, the wedding planner cursed the wedding herself. Seems like it's something she would do. Maybe you should look into *her* first."

Bev didn't want to think about it. "Look, I've got to get back to the inn. Hopefully, the cleric is there, and that'll be one thing off Vicky's mind."

Etheldra looked dubious but waved her off.

Bev had every intention of going to the inn straightaway, but as soon as she emerged from the back room, she stopped short.

Zed was sitting with Lucy and Vicky, holding Vicky's hand and patting it.

"Your dress? Goodness me."

"Just an accident," Lucy said with a small tut. "You know how things can get in the days before a wedding."

"You poor thing," he said, reaching to take her hand before leaning in to sniff the tea. "Good old Etheldra. She's got the thing."

Vicky hiccupped, clearly torn between loyalty to Allen and wanting comfort.

He turned her hand to look at her ring, and Bev's breath caught in her throat.

"Your ring is so beautiful," he said with a kind smile. "Can't imagine how Allen was able to afford something so fine."

"He said he paid a lot for it," Vicky said, her

hysteria easing at the mention of her favorite topic.

"I can tell." He eyed it a little more closely. "Do you know where he got it—"

"I'm not sure," Vicky said, dabbing her nose with the handkerchief. "I—"

"You know, Zed," Bev said, a little too loudly, causing everyone at the table to jump. "Karen told me she needed help setting up the tent. Would you mind?"

Zed squeezed Vicky's hand and gave her an affirming smile. "Sure thing. Happy to be of assistance."

~

Karen seemed to have all she needed for the tent and had found more unwilling participants to set it up, including Sheriff Rustin, Ida, and Valta and her sister Gilda. As before, the event planner was barking orders as each pole went up, and to Bev's gaze, all the ropes were brand new.

"Ah, well, suppose not," Bev said, rubbing the back of her head. "You know that Karen, she finds a way to get what she wants."

"Indeed she does," Zed said, his gaze turning back to the tea shop. "That poor girl. I wonder who she made so angry to have caused such bad luck."

"Erm… Sorry?" Etheldra's words hung heavy in her mind. She still wasn't sure what to think about Zed, especially after seeing him lie so easily about being on Herman's farm. Then again, he could've been telling the truth. It was so hard to tell with him.

"I mean, it seems like some force out there doesn't like her," he said with a laugh. "Figure of speech. Sorry, I suppose there's not much humor in it now, is there?"

"No, I just…" Bev cleared her throat. "Have you had a chance to catch up with Allen?"

He shook his head. "He's so busy right now. I don't want to interrupt him. I'm sure we'll find a few moments closer to the wedding." He let out a contented sigh. "I'm so darn proud of him. This wedding is truly one for the ages, and he's managed to do it all himself. With his fiancée, of course, but…"

"They really have been working hard," Bev said.

"Not only paying for the wedding, but that ring. It looked so expensive." Zed shook his head. "Fernley's was a small little speck in comparison. Vicky's is practically shimmering."

Bev swallowed. Had he noticed the undercurrent of magic? She cursed Allen for not telling Vicky the truth. Clearly, Bev had to *remind* him so Vicky could hide it before Zed realized the truth.

"You know," Bev said, as they walked closer to the inn, "I need to run over to Allen's to talk about…erm…breakfast in the morning."

"Oh, I—"

"Be right back!"

Bev left him there, scurrying across the street to the bakery. The front door was open, but no one was at the counter.

"Allen?"

"In here."

Bev followed his voice into the back room, where he was surrounded by three different sized sponges—some cooling on a rack, some in pans ready for the oven, and even more actually in the oven.

Allen had a large whisk in a bowl of mix that he was stirring rapidly, his face a mask of concentration. "What can I do for you?"

"It certainly smells delicious in here," Bev said with a smile. "Already baking the cake? Shouldn't you do it closer to the wedding?"

"With the icing on, it'll be fine," he said, putting down the bowl and wiping his forehead with the back of his hand. There were purple bags under his eyes, and his shoulders sank heavily as he leaned back against his kitchen table. "What's going on?"

Bev once again found herself the bearer of bad news, and she was starting to dislike that role immensely. "Well, first of all, your bride's dress caught on fire."

Allen let out a soft curse and stared at the ceiling.

"She's fine. Apolinary says it'll be fine," Bev said, quickly. "But she's a mess."

Another weary sigh and nod.

"And more importantly, your father caught up with her at Etheldra's tea shop," Bev said. "And he was very interested in her ring." A pause. "Have you told Vicky where you got it? What it is?"

"No."

Bev pursed her lips. "Why not?"

"Because I've been a *little* busy since I gave it to her," he snapped then seemed to regret it. "And I didn't think it would be a problem." He groaned and put his head in his hands. "What a disaster."

"You need to talk to her about it," Bev said gently. "Maybe she can put it away until Zed leaves town. She could come up with some excuse for needing it resized, or say she were worried, with everything going wrong, that it would disappear."

"I'll figure something out," Allen said. "Thanks, Bev. Sorry I'm a bit on edge. I want to get this cake baked and put together. Then I'll be able to breathe easier."

CHAPTER THIRTEEN

Bev returned to the inn, which was quiet, save Clarice's soft snores by the fire and Biscuit's equally soft snores by her feet. The sound of chopping vegetables and the roast sizzling in the oven was a nice backdrop to her swirling thoughts.

It certainly *felt* like something magical was going on, perhaps to cause just enough trouble to convince the bride and groom to call it off. Every incident was bad enough to cause a ruckus, but not so bad that someone got seriously hurt.

While it was easy to think someone might have it out for Allen or Vicky, the list of suspects there was quite small. If it was truly a curse, Jacob could've cast it and left without a care in the world.

Or, perhaps more likely, an unknown culprit for an unknown reason.

Hendry's pinpointing of Karen had stuck in Bev's mind, but Bev was starting to believe perhaps the planner was the intended target, rather than the culprit. Maybe someone with professional jealousy who wanted to ensure Karen's latest venture went so poorly she could never work again. That meant the culprit was probably back in Middleburg.

Bev certainly hoped not. But perhaps she could ask the wedding planner over dinner if she had any enemies.

Although it would mess up the room arrangements, Bev couldn't help but fervently hope Wallace would be the next person to walk through the door. It might be the thing to change Allen and Vicky's luck. But as Bev brought the dinner spread out from the kitchen, there was a pang of disappointment when she didn't see the cleric among those queued up to eat. Hopefully, he and Paul were just stuck somewhere, and not hurt or something worse.

"How's Vicky?" Bev asked Etheldra, who was first in line.

"She's not hysterical anymore, thanks to the whiskey." Etheldra shook her head. "But she said she was coming to dinner this evening, so you'll be able to see for yourself. I believe she left with her aunt. That one's *somewhat* tolerable, at least."

Bev didn't have an answer for that, as Marion and Nadia came downstairs. The former's gaze swept the dinner spread on the table and, for once, didn't have a derogatory comment. At least not one Bev could hear.

Karen arrived a few moments after that, a large case of wine in hand. She placed it on the table, a confident smile on her face.

"The tent is up and holding, and I've personally tasted all six of these bottles to ensure the utmost quality," she boasted, her gaze squarely on Marion. "I believe that this wedding is going to go off without a hitch now!"

"Assuming Apolinary can fix Vicky's dress," Marion said with a sigh. "Goodness knows she's slow."

Karen's eye began twitching. "I'm sorry… What happened to Vicky's dress?"

"It caught on fire," Nadia muttered, pushing a piece of potato from side to side.

Karen's face shifted. "*What*?"

"Caught fire," Nadia said, looking like the idea gave her a little glee. "The seamstress said it was a freak accident with glass and sunlight."

Karen nodded, as if the information wasn't making sense to her. "Sure. I've heard that." She cleared her throat. "Where is Vicky?"

"With Lucy, I imagine, with that *dreadful* seamstress Alice Mary or whatever her name is,"

Marion said, taking a long drink of wine. "*We* spent the afternoon with the far superior one, Rosie. Such a delight. And her chickens! So well behaved."

Bev almost choked.

"Well, I should probably go check on her," Karen said, backing up slowly, almost like she wasn't sure what to do. "I'm sure everything is fine. But you know. Just for moral support. Probably gave her a fright."

She scampered from the room.

Etheldra leveled a look at Bev that was clear. Bev sighed.

And followed her.

Bev didn't have to go far. Karen and Vicky were visible in the lamplight of the bakery next door, concern on both their faces. Lucy was there, too, watching Vicky with pursed lips. Allen was seated in the corner, his arms folded across his chest. There didn't seem to be a smile in the place. Bev didn't want to intrude, but she *did* have a good excuse for barging in.

"Knock, knock," she said, opening the door with a smile as if she couldn't sense the tension in the room. "Just wanted to check if you lot are coming by for dinner."

Whatever argument they'd been in the middle of abruptly ceased, and based on Allen's expression, he was grateful for the interruption.

"I'm coming," he said gruffly.

"We're all going," Karen said, her expression too bright. "Come, Vicky."

"I'm not hungry," she said, pouting. "Don't want to face Aunt Marion and hear about how so-and-so was *much* better at handling things when *her* dress caught on fire."

"Marion means well," Lucy said, patting Vicky on the back helpfully. "She's a bit...well, I don't think she hears herself sometimes. But she gave you that bracelet, didn't she?" Lucy patted it. "She held onto it for you. She does love you, deep down."

Vicky gave Lucy a half-smile. "You're right. It is a lovely bracelet."

"There, now. All will be right with a spot of dinner," Karen said. "Chin up, Vicky. Let's get you back over to the inn and have some wine. I personally tasted the two bottles and can assure you they're both excellent."

"Were you able to get the tent back up?" Bev asked.

"Indeed, we were," Karen replied, glancing at Bev as if she were an annoying gnat. "Nothing a good bit of rope can't fix. I tell you, I've done a hundred weddings in my career, and they *all* have their mishaps. Poor Petunia Greenblatt—the whole altar caught on fire during her wedding." Karen let out a loud laugh. "Scared everyone half to death, but I tell you: they've been happily married for five years now with four beautiful children, so the worse the chaos, the better the marriage. I'd be more worried if nothing *had* gone wrong." She patted Vicky's cheek. "You're handling it all beautifully, dear. Now, let's get you across the street. A nice glass of wine will loosen your nerves."

Slowly, Vicky nodded and headed across the street, Lucy right on her heels. Karen lingered in the doorway and gave Allen a sideways look, her chipper demeanor fading into a scowl.

"And I expect *you* to buck up, understand?" she said, sounding harsher than she had all week. "Nobody likes a grumpy groom."

The door slammed behind her, leaving Allen and Bev alone.

"Well, she's a character," Bev said, breaking the silence. "Are you all right, Allen?"

"Fine," he mumbled, looking as morose and defeated as he had when he was bartering away his meager earnings for a bit of his mother's magic from the barus.

And in fact…

"Is that Vicky's ring?" Bev asked, noting the green bauble in his hand. "You got it?"

He pointed to a bruise on his head. "Yeah, I got it all right. She wasn't too happy I asked for it back."

Bev licked her lips. "You did tell her *why* you wanted it back, didn't you?"

"Absolutely not," he said with a scowl. "I don't want her to know. Remember?"

Bev closed her eyes and pinched the bridge of her nose. *Silly man.* "Allen…"

"I asked her if I could hold onto it for her. And of course, because it's *Vicky*, she thought I was asking…" He huffed. "Well, I think you can connect the dots."

Bev frowned. "She thought you wanted to call off the wedding?"

"I don't, obviously," he said, though Bev had a hard time believing that. "But I don't know. Maybe I should. Pretty sure this is some kind of sign. Jacob was probably right."

"It's not a sign," Bev said, a little helplessly.

"The bride's dress caught on fire. That's a pretty big sign." Allen crossed his arms again. "Not to mention, the cleric's not here. The tent fell down. The wine. The flowers. My father being here."

Bev crossed the room to stand next to him. "Allen, this isn't like you. What's going on? Are you getting cold feet?"

"It's everything," he said with a sigh. "Jacob tells me I shouldn't marry her and refuses to be in the wedding. Then my father shows up, acting like he's here for a reconciliation, but then he disappears all day. Now we have mishap after mishap for this giant wedding I don't even *want*, and…" He rubbed his face. "Every piece of gold I've made the past two months has gone out the door. And I've been working my tail off to pay for it all this week. But no, if you talk to *Key-ran*, I'm not a happy groom. I need to be cheerful for my bride, as she's under a lot of stress. What about me, eh?"

Bev squeezed his hand. "You're allowed to be a, what did she call you? A grumpy groom."

He cracked a smile and squeezed her hand back. "Glad I have you in my corner, Bev."

"This, erm, *Key-ran* as you call her," Bev said, looking around the bakery. "What's your sense about her?"

"Hm?" He furrowed his brow for a moment before responding. "Overbearing. Intense. Thinks I'm superfluous to the whole event."

"I see."

"Why?"

"You know, everything that's gone wrong—save Vicky's dress—has been something of hers," Bev said. "The wine. The flower food. Even the tent ropes. I'm wondering…"

"You don't think she's doing it intentionally?" Allen asked. "Why?"

"Perhaps to show Vicky's aunts what a capable event manager she is?" Bev suggested. "That or someone's out to get her and ruin her reputation. But I can't get more than two words with her to find out."

"She does save her praises for those she thinks

are worthy," Allen said with a dry laugh. "Vicky says she's quite the planner. Came with impeccable references, too." He paused, tapping his fingers on the counter. "You know, it was honestly a little bit suspect that she agreed to come here and manage our wedding."

"Why?"

"She's used to planning events for people like Nadia. Folks with loads of gold and connections and standing in much bigger cities," Allen said. "I asked myself a few times what she might gain from doing our ceremony."

"Interesting." Bev's gaze crossed the street to the inn, where presumably Karen was regaling the audience with the story of how she'd single-handedly saved the wedding. "I'm not saying it's not a string of bad luck, either. But it does seem suspect."

"I mean, I don't think it means we're going to have a happy marriage," Allen said, sounding a little distant.

"What?" Bev turned to him. "What do you mean?"

"Nothing." He gave her a fake smile. "Let's eat. I'm famished."

~

True to form, by the time Allen and Bev returned to the inn, Karen was regaling the crowd, or better yet, Marion, with the tale of how she demanded another crate of wine from the vintner, and how she *wasn't* going to take no for an answer.

"They tasted it and said it was fine, but I *know* what I tasted the night before," Karen said, oblivious to the way Etheldra was glowering at her. "You can't pull a fast one on me. I've been doing this *too* long." She paused, but only to catch her breath. "A few years ago, I had something similar happen at the wedding of Shelly Richards. The vintner tried to sell me some terrible wine, then, too," Karen said with a wink. "Everyone thought they could pull a fast one on me, but I tell you, I know better! Always had good instincts on these sorts of things, you know?"

"Indeed, I do." Marion puffed out her chest. "I also have good business instincts."

"I can tell," Karen said with an overenthusiastic nod.

Allen caught Bev's gaze, and they shared a knowing smile as the two women boasted of their respective accolades. Bev scrutinized the planner, still unable to decide which side of the mystery she lay on. Villain or victim?

Karen had continued telling Marion all about Shelly Richards's wedding, but the other woman cut her short.

"Dear me, I must've missed that particular society article," Marion said. Bev felt a thrill of victory that the Sheepsburg denizen didn't seem too impressed with the wedding planner. "I will say, you've done quite well for all the chaos that comes from a rural wedding like this."

"I do love a challenge," Karen said with a flourishing laugh.

"This wedding has been the definition of that," Marion said. "Though I suppose we can put the blame on young Grant. Can't believe he skipped town the way he did. I told Nadia that boy is destined for a hard life if he doesn't get himself together."

She continued ranting about Grant being a ne'er-do-well, to the point that even Bev wanted to stick up for the boy. But she didn't want to draw Marion's attention, so she kept quiet.

Etheldra grumbled as she picked up her plate and brought it to Bev. "Can you believe this? The two of them have been going on since they walked in the door." She sniffed in Karen's direction. "I still believe there's something funny with that woman. You looked into her yet?"

"Not quite," Bev said. "Been focused on other things."

The thing Bev had been focused on walked in, his boots covered in mud and his uniform showing clear signs he'd been out in the bushes. Bev hadn't seen him again after leaving him to speak to Allen a few hours ago, and clearly, he'd been doing... something. But the bright smile on his face showed no signs that he'd been traipsing through anything.

"Evening, folks," Zed announced, as Marion rose dramatically. Karen was all but forgotten beside her, and Bev couldn't help but notice how the event planner scowled at being demoted to second place in Marion's eyes.

"You look a sight, Zed," Marion practically fawned over him. "Where have you been all day?"

"Looking around at my old stomping grounds," he said. "I used to work the fields out west before I joined the queen's service. Thought it would be nice to feel the dirt under my boots again. Something about this place is quite grounding, you know?"

Allen scoffed, spearing a potato with his fork and cramming it into his mouth.

"Well, we've had quite the eventful day," Marion said, regaling Zed with a much-embellished tale about how the light came in at the right angle and set Vicky's dress on fire.

"I caught up with her earlier today," Zed said with a nod. "How are you doing, sweetheart?"

"No worse for the wear," Vicky said weakly. "I think I might retire, though. We've got a busy day tomorrow, and I'm absolutely exhausted."

"And I've got to get the cake put together," Allen said, rising slowly.

"Oh, sod the cake, Allen," Vicky said, her happy demeanor slipping after the day she'd had. "We're going to eat it anyway. Why does it matter what it looks like?"

"The same reason it matters that your dress is perfect," he snapped. "I'm sure Apolinary won't be sleeping, so why should we?"

"You know, it's been a long day for the two of you," Karen said, walking between them. "I think it's best you both go home and get some rest. Allen, you can finish your cake in the morning, can't you? Or that assistant can, right?"

He glowered, but perhaps his own tiredness won over. "Fine. I'm going home."

But before they could walk out the door, it opened, and two figures strode in with bright smiles on their faces.

"Ah, Bev!" Wallace cheered. "Glad to see you once more. Where's the happy couple?"

Chapter Fourteen

Wallace the cleric was bald, with dark brown skin and a casual air. His husband Paul's hair was shorter than it had been at the solstice, and he looked a little less uptight than he'd been last time he'd stayed at the inn. Perhaps the past few months had been kinder to them.

Wallace crossed the room to embrace Bev, and she returned it with gusto.

"So happy you two made it," Bev said. "I was getting a bit worried."

"Eh?" Wallace frowned and turned to Paul. "Why?"

"Well, Vicky said we expected you days ago," Bev said.

"Oh, we got sidetracked a bit at Kaiser Tuckey's!" Wallace waved her off, and Bev got the distinct impression they *were* late. "Now, where can I find the happy couple?"

Vicky stepped forward with a smile, grabbing Allen's arm roughly and yanking him toward her.

"Ah, yes. What a handsome pair," Wallace said. "And so young. You two are going to have a long, happy life together, eh?"

"We certainly hope so," Vicky said, her voice too high.

"Yeah," Allen added as an afterthought.

"Ah. Well." Wallace put his hands into his pockets, and Bev could practically read his mind. "You know, as a matter of course, before I marry anyone, I like to do a little counseling session. Just a few questions to make sure you've really thought this out. Most everyone sails right through, no problems. But it's always good to start a marriage on the right foot." He nodded to Paul. "Right, my love?"

Paul nodded, but his gaze was on Bev. "Our room has been paid for, yes?"

Bev started. "Yes, it has, but we do need to do a bit of rearranging." She thanked her lucky stars she had some clean sheets on standby. "Erm. Marion, Lucy—"

"So this is the lovely cleric who'll be marrying the children," Marion said, ignoring Bev's entreaties.

"Mrs. Marion Bilensbrook. Charmed to meet you."

Wallace took her hand and shook it gently. "Likewise. You are…?"

"Vicky's *eldest* aunt, and the only thing keeping this wedding from careening off a hill!" Marion said with a laugh. "It's such a good thing I've been here."

"Erm, yes," Vicky said, with an apologetic look to Karen. "Wallace, this is my other aunt, Lucy, and my cousin, Nadia, Marion's daughter." She pointed around the room. "This is—"

"Ah, Ms. Etheldra." Wallace smiled thinly. "Good to see you again."

"Harrumph," Etheldra said with a glare. "Hope you aren't planning to get into the drink again. We've had plenty of trouble with that as it is."

Vicky ignored Etheldra and continued introducing Wallace to everyone, including Clarice, who rose to shake the cleric's hand with a bright smile. Zed, introduced as Allen's father, waved from across the room. The last one was Karen, who also took Wallace's hand with a firm shake.

"Pardon, you said your name was…?" he said.

"Karen Mayhew," she said. "I'm a wedding planner out of Middleburg."

He eyed her for a moment before the suspicion disappeared from his face. "Wonderful to meet you. I trust Vicky's in good hands with you at her side."

"Indeed, she is," Karen said.

"Well, we are *all* so happy you could make it,"

Marion said, butting into the conversation again. "Please, tell me your background. You're obviously *experienced* in the matter of weddings and the like, are you not?"

Wallace, to his credit, didn't blink at the question. "I've been a cleric for these past thirty years," he said. "It's truly my calling, especially dealing with interpersonal conflicts." He caught Bev's gaze, which then dropped to his still-empty hand. "But I do love officiating weddings as well. We spent a few days in Pigsend over the last winter solstice, and when I received the letter from Allen that he was looking for someone, we absolutely jumped at the chance to return to the Weary Dragon." He sighed as he looked around. "It's such a lovely little place."

"I'm sure you've been to larger inns with much more to offer," Marion drawled before Bev could thank Wallace for his kind words.

"True, but none with an innkeeper with as much heart," Wallace finished. "Bev truly is one of a kind, you know."

"Hear, hear," Allen said.

"Thirded," Etheldra, of all people, spoke up as well.

Bev put her hand to her chest, taken aback by the nice words. "Well, I can't say I'm anything special, but I do appreciate the kindness."

Marion ignored the conversation. "Thirty years

as a cleric! You certainly do get around, then, don't you? What is your area of ministry?"

"We tend to bounce around this part of the country," Wallace said. "Kaiser Tuckey is a common patron. Are you familiar with him?"

Marion's eyes flashed, and Bev could practically see the wheels turning. "I can't say that I am."

"He's got quite the manor," Vicky said. "Perhaps a day's ride from here."

Bev could practically hear the undertone. *He's rich, Aunt Marion. So he's worth your interest.*

"Ah, well. Must pay him a visit next time I'm in town," Marion said, brushing her hands on her dress. "I do believe it's getting late. Nadia, we must return to our rooms to get our beauty rest."

Bev cleared her throat. "About that. Marion—"

"*Mrs. Bilensbrook*, dear. We've discussed this."

"Mrs. Bilensbrook," Bev said with a weary sigh. "Either you or Ms. Lucy or Ms. Nadia will have to move rooms so we'll have a place for Paul and Wallace to sleep."

"Well, why in the world is that?" Marion asked. "Is it your poor planning that—"

"Actually, I believe it's my fault," Zed said, raising his hand.

"Oh, dear Zed, how could you possibly be the cause of this?" Immediately, Marion's face shifted into a sycophantic smile, and Bev was actually grateful for his presence.

"I don't think Ms. Bev was planning on having me," he said, a little sheepishly. "So I somewhat strong-armed her into giving me a room."

"Surely, there's someone else who can—" Marion began.

Lucy sighed and rose. "I'm happy to be the one to move. Nadia and I can share. She won't mind, will you, love?"

Nadia looked like she *would* mind but didn't argue. Marion, too, looked affronted on her daughter's behalf, but kept her mouth shut, presumably as Zed's gaze was still on her.

"That's settled, then," Bev said. "Let me help you move your things, Ms. Lucy. Then we'll get the room reset, and Wallace and Paul will be able to rest their heads. Give me fifteen minutes to get it all sorted."

"Oh, let me help," Wallace said, picking up the suitcase. "I insist."

It didn't take long to move Lucy's things, especially with Wallace's assistance. She had one trunk that was already tidied and put away, almost like she'd been expecting this turn of events. Bev thanked her again for her flexibility, and Lucy waved her off.

"After the day Vicky's had, I'm grateful to take something off her plate," she said. "And I'm glad our cleric has arrived so we can have a wedding, at least."

"Erm. Yes." Wallace rubbed his chin. "Me, too."

Bev didn't question the hesitation in his voice until they were back in the room, stripping the bed and putting on new sheets.

"What's the matter?" Bev asked, hoping against hope that nothing *had* gone wrong, like Wallace losing his ability to perform marriages. That, of course, seemed far-fetched, but so had Vicky's dress catching on fire.

"Well, the couple, they don't seem…" He chuckled. "They don't seem very *happy,* do they?"

"Oh." Bev almost heaved a sigh of relief. That, at least, she could answer. "Well, goodness, they've both had a stressful couple of days." She gave him the rundown of all the mishaps, and his eyes widened when she got to the part about Vicky's dress.

"They have had a rough go of it, haven't they?" Wallace said. "But you know what they say about bad luck and all that. Still, what you've described seems to take the cake." He chuckled. "Pun intended."

"I've half a mind to think some of this is the machinations of that wedding planner," Bev said, lowering her voice. "She seems too eager to impress and might be causing trouble just to solve it."

"Erm, yes. I did notice her." He rubbed the back of his head. "Surprised to see her, actually."

Bev frowned. "Why?"

"Well, I've done a lot of weddings all over the place," he said. "Including in Turtleville."

"Where's that?"

"About three days' ride north of here," he said. "I wasn't sure it was her until she introduced herself, but I'd recognize that name anywhere—and I have seen her, though it seems she's forgotten my face." He paused. "Now, I don't know all the details, but from what I gathered, about a year ago, a bride there had paid Karen a large sum to manage her wedding. Everything was going swimmingly until Karen disappeared two days before." Wallace gave her a look. "Didn't refund her money, didn't even offer an apology. Just flat-out disappeared."

"And now she's here," Bev said. "Maybe she *is* the problem. I wonder how I could confront her about it?"

"I haven't a clue," he said. "But I'll be sure to mention it to the bride and groom. Forewarned is forearmed, in any case." He sighed and looked around the room. "You know, I daresay I missed this place. Even with all the excitement at the end of our stay." He tilted his head. "Have we heard any more from Bernie?"

"No." Bev was glad for that. "Dag Flanigan's been by a few more times. His, er… His boss is here now. Zed. Allen's father."

Wallace paled a little, and his fingers danced

near where he used to wear his magical ring. "I see. Just in town for the wedding?"

"Hard to say," Bev replied. "So if you've managed to find any more of those little magical rings, you might want to hide them."

He gave Bev a tight smile. "No more of those for me, I'm afraid. It was so rare to begin with. And, to be honest, the whole ordeal scared Paul half to death. He gave me a chewing out over it, I'll tell you what." He paused. "I've also given up the ale, you'll be happy to hear."

Bev was, if only because she hadn't accounted for the cleric's drinking habits. "I'm happy that you're safe and sound. You two have a good night."

Bev returned downstairs, earning a heartfelt thank you from Paul, who went upstairs to join his husband. The front room had emptied out now, with the regulars gone, as well as Vicky and Allen. Marion had presumably retired to her room, and Nadia was already in her room with Lucy. Bev was grateful she didn't have to do any more smoothing over, though she had a hunch she'd hear more about it in the morning.

Karen was still downstairs, surprisingly, as was Zed, and the two were having a nice conversation about the plan for the wedding. Bev let them have their chat, dipping into the kitchen to do the dishes and the other tasks she needed to complete before finally retiring for the night. She kept the door to the kitchen propped so she could hear, and perhaps get more insight into their *real* purpose in town.

As she scrubbed, the only topics were the wedding, the plan for the day, and how Karen was going to execute the all-day event with finesse. Since Marion wasn't in earshot, she left out much of the bravado Bev was used to hearing, but she was still clearly trying to make a good impression on him, as well. It seemed the only one she *didn't* want to speak to at length was Bev, perhaps because the only unmarried people Bev knew were about to be married in four days' time.

"You've certainly got this down to an art, haven't you?" Zed said.

"If you do anything enough times, you tend to be able to anticipate the things that go wrong," she said. "To be honest, this is one of the smaller weddings I've managed. Some of the bigger ones have lasted a full week!"

Zed chuckled. "When Fernley and I got married, it was under a little peach tree out on the farm."

"That's right, you were saying you were from here," Karen said, glancing at his boots. "Well, I can't say Allen has given me instruction on how he wants to include you in the wedding, but I'll be sure to find a place for you."

Zed waved her off. "No need. We have

something of a fraught relationship."

"Allen's being a grump. Many of my grooms get that way in the days before the wedding. I've done hundreds of these, and everything always works out in the end."

"Everyone is in good hands," Zed said. "I'm glad to be here to witness it, even if my son doesn't want me to be."

Bev slowed her scrubbing, listening intently.

"Might I ask what went south?" Karen asked. "As a wedding planner, I've often found myself helping with these interpersonal problems."

"Well, I'm sure he's not too pleased I left him and his mother a few years ago," he said. "Perhaps even less pleased that I joined the queen's service after the war."

Bev started. *After?*

"You've got quite the rank for only having been in for a few years," Karen said.

"Started my career on the king's side," he said. "Found success by offering up some of the worst offenders in the war." He shook his head. "I really soured on a lot of what we did, so I felt it was making up for the sins of the king's army."

Bev chewed her lip. That certainly could explain how he'd ended up managing a man like Dag Flanigan. But she sincerely hoped Vellora didn't catch wind of his treachery. She'd probably have to leave town to keep her anger in check.

"I...see..." Even Karen sounded dubious about his turncoat nature.

"Sometimes, you have to see the writing on the wall," he said. "When it became clear we were going to lose, and badly, I switched my allegiance and ended up on the better side of things. Have a nice career I can be proud of looking for some of the most dangerous practitioners of magic."

And are you here looking for one now? Bev thought with bated breath.

But if he was, he didn't offer that up. "Unfortunately, that career meant I had to leave everything and everyone behind. Fernley and I didn't really get along by the time I left, of course, but I always felt awful about leaving Allen. I tried to write often, but..."

"Well," Karen said, after a long pause, "perhaps we can't hope for a full reconciliation, but we can come to understand one another. You clearly still care about your son, so we can start there and see. Maybe making up with you will put him in a better frame of mind."

Bev had to scowl a little. Karen sure was picking on Allen, and Bev didn't like it too much.

"One can only hope."

Bev needed to return to the front room to grab the rest of the dirty dishes, and this time, she couldn't avoid Zed's gaze as he beamed at her.

"Are we all set upstairs?" he asked. "I hope my

arrival didn't cause too much of a stir with Ms. Marion."

"Depends if you're around when she talks to me about it," Bev said with a dark chuckle. "We're all set now. If any other long-lost relatives come knocking, I'll have to send them down the road to Middleburg."

CHAPTER FIFTEEN

Bev awoke the next morning feeling like the winds had shifted a little. Wallace's arrival, even if he didn't think the happy couple looked too happy, was the last piece of the puzzle. Now, even if everything else went haywire, the two could get married.

She still wasn't quite sure about Karen, and although there wasn't *much* she could do, she did vow to keep an eye on the wedding planner, in case. Perhaps with constant supervision, Bev might be able to circumvent anything else going wrong.

Unfortunately, Karen was up and out the door even before the muffins arrived, the only sign of her presence the slamming of the front door. While Bev couldn't leave the inn before her guests came down, she did have a furry little backup plan.

"Keep an eye on her today, will you, Biscuit?" she said to her laelaps, who wagged his tail in affirmation. "If she does anything funny, come get me."

She opened the front door, and Biscuit put his nose to the ground, walking off the way Karen had gone, and Bev returned to her bread dough.

But she hadn't gotten through a full minute of kneading before Zed walked down the stairs. He caught sight of Bev through the open kitchen door and waved, joining her inside.

"Morning."

"Morning," Bev said with a nod. "Sleep all right?"

"Oh, yes, of course." Another smile. "I wanted to thank you again for your flexibility."

"Don't thank me. Thank Lucy," Bev said, working the dough.

Zed watched her for a minute. "It's amazing how this place runs exactly the same. And yet, everything is different." He nodded to the front door. "Am I to guess that you remodeled the entire front door of the inn?"

"Ah, yes," Bev said. "Though not by choice." She told him the story of Karolina Hunter's team coming to town, stopping the magical river that flowed beneath the surface, and causing earthquakes and sinkholes. She spared no detail, including how Karolina was content to let someone else take the blame for the trouble she'd caused (though she left out that the someone else was a six-foot moleman who lived beneath the surface), hoping to glean something from his response.

He let out a sigh. "What a mess. I'm glad things didn't turn out worse for you."

"Almost did," Bev said. "The Brewer twins lost their home, and Stella was injured. But what I can't wrap my head around was that a queen's soldier—someone who supposedly was in town to help—not only *knew* their actions were endangering townsfolk but said nothing about it." She waited, giving him a sideways look.

"Some soldiers can be like that," he said, much to Bev's disappointment. "I'd be happy to find her superior officer and let them know what she did."

"Somehow, I get the feeling they know, and they condoned it," Bev said.

He tutted, but it was still good-natured. "You sound a tad bitter, Bev."

She gave him a look. "I lost the front of my inn, Zed. People got hurt. The whole town was on edge. And it was only because *I* found the contraption—"

"You found it?" His eyebrows rose. "How did you find it?"

Bev realized too late what he was doing—perhaps. It was ridiculously difficult to read Zed.

One moment, she was convinced he was a remorseful absent father, who'd chosen career over family and who'd come to regret it. The next, he seemed keen to uncover something Bev didn't want him to uncover.

"I found it at the edge of Alice Estrich's farm," Bev said, after a long pause. "Large, black, gaudy thing. Surprised no one else found it."

"Over near the dark forest, yeah?" Zed asked. "How on earth did you know what it was? And for that matter, how did you find the magical river?"

"The gnomes told me," Bev said, choosing her words carefully. "They were over near Dane Sterling's farm, digging for magic, so I assume. They told me they were looking for magic for Her Majesty, but they couldn't find any." She paused. "Seemed a bit like a miscommunication. One group of the queen's people in town to stop the river, the other looking for it."

"That does happen. The queen's got a lot of folks working for her." He tapped on the table. "Bread looks good. Can't wait to have a slice later."

"Where are you off to?" Bev asked, hoping she sounded nonchalant.

"Here and there." He disappeared out the door, leaving Bev to wonder if she'd sent Biscuit to follow the wrong person.

But as soon as that thought crossed her mind, Biscuit pawed open the back door and barked at her.

"Did you find her?" Bev asked.

He let out a low ruff.

She sighed and untied her apron. "Suppose this bread's done enough. Let's go see what Karen's up to."

~

Biscuit led her out of town, going north—toward the dark forest, of all places. She'd almost forgotten the place existed, having not been there since the solstice. The forest was somewhat sentient and had a high concentration of magic, and had Biscuit not proven himself to be highly intelligent, Bev might've assumed he was taking her to the forest to eat a juicy morsel.

But he kept going as Bev crossed under the threshold into the forest. The leaves rustled as if moved by the wind, but the forest didn't seem to tear at her clothes the way it had once upon a time. Perhaps it was Biscuit's presence, or perhaps it was feeling friendly today, but it let Bev walk through easily until she spotted Karen up ahead.

The event planner stood in a clearing, her black tunic almost blending in with the dark trees behind her. She was staring at her time piece on a chain, tapping her foot. In her other hand was a large money bag.

Bev crouched behind a bush before Karen noticed her. "Good job, Biscuit."

Biscuit sniffed beside her.

"What do you reckon she's doing here?" Bev whispered. "Hopefully, not running afoul of Zed."

Pop!

A creature appeared on a stump next to Karen.

"The barus!" Bev whispered to herself.

The creature, who probably came up to Bev's hip, had large ears that folded over like a dog's and a short, piggy snout complete with bright pink skin. He gave Karen the same sort of bored stare he'd given Allen all those months ago. Dealing with him was a recipe for disaster, in Bev's experience, anyway, and she couldn't fathom why Karen had summoned him.

"You're late," Karen snapped. "I've been waiting for an hour."

"These kinds of things don't travel well," he drawled, sounding uninterested that he'd caused her angst. "And I do expect to be paid for my trouble."

"Twenty gold coins, as discussed," Karen said, her voice taking on an uncharacteristic note of worry. She clutched the money bag in her hand. "I want to see it first."

He sniffed, reaching inside his tunic and to retrieve something small. He handed it to her, and she greedily opened it, peering inside.

Biscuit's nose immediately perked up.

"And you're sure this will work?" she said. "I'm paying a lot of money for this thing. And risking my neck. There's a soldier in town who'd throw me in jail for having it."

"Aye. It's the real deal. Took it from a leprechaun myself." He cracked a grin. "Unfortunately, it'll only work for the next three days, so if you're wanting more—"

"Two days is all I need," she said, holding the small bag as if it were the most precious thing in the world to her. "Then I'm chucking it as far as I can."

Bev's eyes widened. *It's for the wedding?*

"Do what you like," he said, holding out his outstretched hand. "Now, the twenty-five gold—"

"Twenty-five?" She started. "You said twenty."

"It took me a while to get. Lots of soldiers on the road." He chuckled. "Five extra gold for insurance, you know."

She growled, but reached into her pocket and handed him more gold. "This thing had better work. Or else."

"My reputation precedes me," he said with a flourish. "Now if there's nothing else…"

He disappeared with a *pop*.

Karen stood there for a moment, staring at the item in the bag, before closing it, pocketing it with a satisfied nod then heading toward the forest edge. Bev was well-hidden enough that Karen walked right by her without noticing, but once she was through, Bev popped up and followed at a distance, Biscuit at her heels. What sort of magic had the barus procured for Karen? Allen, of course, had been seeking to replicate his mother's pobyd magic and had racked up a large debt to pay for it. What he hadn't understood, but Karen clearly did, was that the magic the barus provided was enough to get one going but it would run out. When it did, the barus banked on the person returning to get more, at which point, the creature would exact a higher price. And so it went, until the person was drowning in debt.

Karen, it seemed, knew better. The wedding was tomorrow, after all, so that had to be what she needed this bit of magic for. Was she planning on using it to heroically save the wedding in front of Marion? If so, she was gambling on Zed not noticing, something Bev wasn't sure would be the case.

Karen didn't slow, even when she got to town. She made a beeline for the tent, which was blessedly still up, and headed underneath. Inside, there was a stack of chairs and tables that must've been delivered sometime the day before, and Karen let out a loud breath as she reached into her pocket, presumably to hold the thing she'd gotten from the barus.

But she seemed to sense Bev's presence, and spun around with a too-bright smile.

"H-Hi, Bev," Karen said, recovering from her shock quickly as her face twitched. "I'm quite busy here, so if you need something, make it quick."

Bev watched her for a moment, trying to decide

what she wanted to ask first before finally settling on the question she was most curious about. "Can you tell me what happened in Turtleville?"

Her eyes widened, then almost too late, tried to hide it. "I'm sorry, who?"

"The town of Turtleville. I heard you started your career there," Bev continued.

She gave a half-smile. "Oh? Who did you hear that from?"

"Doesn't matter," Bev said. "Because I also heard you skipped out on a wedding that had already paid you."

She let out a snort of laughter. "I fail to see why this merits a conversation."

"Because I want to make sure *you* aren't the one causing trouble for my dear friends," Bev said, pointing her finger at Karen. "As it's clear you have a history of causing trouble. What was the problem there? Was the bride lacking in connected relatives?"

Karen clicked her tongue, and when she spoke, it was almost as if her voice had evaporated. "It wasn't like that."

"Oh? Then what was it like?"

"The bride was…" She cleared her throat. "Well, I realized she wasn't the sort of person I wanted to be working for. She told me if I left, she'd ruin me. Said I'd never work in Turtleville again. So I cut my losses, left town with what I could carry, and started new in Middleburg." She let out a mirthless chuckle. "Figured that was far enough away that my tarnished reputation couldn't follow. But clearly not."

"I haven't told Vicky or Marion or anyone," Bev said. "But I need to know: are *you* behind any of it?"

"Do you *honestly* think I'd jeopardize this golden opportunity like that?" Karen exclaimed. "Marion Bilensbrook is one of the most well-connected women in Sheepsburg. A good recommendation from her, and my entire career is back on track. I need this wedding to *go well*." She wrung her hands. "Let's just say rebuilding my career in Middleburg isn't going quite as well as I'd hoped, and I fear this is my last chance. So I need Allen to buck up and not look like he's about to go to prison. I need Vicky to stop getting hysterical over every little thing. And most importantly, I need all these little *mishaps* to *stop happening*."

"Don't we all," Bev said with a chuckle then paused. "If that's the case, what did you get from the barus?"

She gave a tight smile and reached into her pocket, pulling out a green bauble. It was a different shade than the one Vicky wore on her finger and gave off a different sort of feel. Almost like fresh mint. "It's a bit of luck."

"Luck?" Bev frowned.

She nodded. "I know what I said about bad weddings and good marriages, but it's starting to feel a little personal at this point. So I asked Allen where he got his bauble from, managed to get a message to the barus, and, well..." She closed her hand around it. "Took all the money I have left to pay for it. But if this works, hopefully, I'll be on my way." She gave Bev a sideways look. "Don't tell anyone. Especially not Allen's father."

"Your secret's safe with me. I'm relieved to find out you're trying to save the wedding."

She blanched. "What other possibility could there be?"

Bev didn't want to tell her the other theory she'd been considering. "What did that bride do that was so awful?"

"It wasn't her, per se," she said softly. "It was her father. He was quite rich, which is why they hired me in the first place. It turned out he'd been responsible for a great deal of pain during the war. I won't go into detail, because it's too gruesome, but needless to say..." She licked her lips. "I'm actually somewhat grateful Allen doesn't seem to like his father."

Bev nodded. "I confess I was listening to your conversation last night. I don't even know if Allen knows all that his father did in the war, but—"

"If he did, I'm sure he'd demand his father leave." Karen eyed her. "Suppose you fought in it? Kingside?"

Bev let out a cough as memories threatened to

come to the surface. "No idea, actually. I'm sure Vicky told you—"

"Right, right. No memories." She chuckled. "Lucky. It was bad in Turtleville. Used to be a beautiful oasis, filled to the brim with all manner of magical creatures. Then, almost overnight, it was completely different. I thought I could look the other way, but..." She cleared her throat. "Well. I made my bed. Now I have to see if I can salvage my career."

"Marion likes you, in any case, and she doesn't seem to like many people," Bev said. "Except Zed."

"Yeah, funny thing, that," Karen said with a sideways glance. "Marion's the sort who wants to ingratiate herself with the highest ranks of society. Allen's father is a decorated war hero, for sure, but out here, military rank isn't quite as important as it is back in the city. So I'm not quite sure why she's so eager to impress him. Can't see the benefit to her, you know?"

Bev frowned. "You don't think *she* might be behind all this trouble, do you?"

"I honestly don't know." Karen shrugged. "She's my ticket to a better career, so I won't say a bad word about her. But it certainly looks like she might be compensating for something."

"She's not the only one acting strangely," Bev said. "I'm not entirely sure Zed doesn't have an ulterior motive for his presence in town. He hadn't spoken to Allen in years, then shows up out of the blue?"

"That's actually somewhat common," Karen said with a small chuckle.

"But he keeps disappearing and coming to the inn with mud all over his boots. I get the feeling he's hiding something, too."

Karen sighed, checking her timepiece. "The day's getting away from me. Lots to do before the festivities tomorrow. Then we can all breathe a little easier."

Chapter Sixteen

The revelations about Karen made Bev feel somewhat more confident about the wedding. The barus was a sneaky creature, but the magic it provided, at least initially, was good. If Karen had a bit of luck on her, maybe things were finally turning around.

She did find it curious that Allen hadn't mentioned talking with Karen about the barus, so before returning to the inn, Bev walked across the street to the bakery. But when she opened the door, Lillie was the only one hard at work.

"Hey there, Bev," Lillie said, her shirt sleeves rolled up to her elbows and her hands deep in a large bowl. "How's it going over there?"

"Oh, fine, fine," Bev said, scenting something sweet in the air. "What are you making?"

"Wedding cookies," she replied, nodding to a card on the table that Bev picked up. "Fernley's recipe."

The handwriting was familiar—Fernley's—and the ingredient list was quite short but included one amusing item.

"Almond flour?"

"Can you believe it?" Lillie said, pulling up a piece of the dough to show her. It was light brown, with flecks of darker brown throughout. "I about lost it when I saw the card. Allen said his mother used to make them along with the cake for every wedding they catered. He said she always wanted to make them for his special day." She beamed, a little color in her cheeks. "It's a wonderful recipe."

"And Allen let you make them?" Bev asked.

"I insisted. He was dead on his feet this morning," Lillie said. "Bad enough he was intent on making his own wedding cake. I told him I couldn't dream of letting him make the cookies, too. And besides that, he's off on another delivery this morning."

"Where to?"

"Not too far, so he should be back by mid-morning," she said. "We've got to finish decorating the cake today. I've done some piping, but I wanted to wait until Allen got back to make sure I had everything right. We spent all day yesterday on it."

"Goodness," Bev said with a laugh. "But the wedding is tomorrow?"

Lillie nodded. "When I used to cater weddings, we'd get the cake ready a day or two ahead of time. Since we assume Vicky will have Allen tied up with all manner of pre-wedding things, we went ahead and got it done. Plus, we still have lots more to bake, including these wedding cookies, a few tarts, some pies—"

"You two are doing too much," Bev said.

"Allen says he's the town baker," Lillie said with a sigh. "And he would be embarrassed if he didn't give his own wedding his best showing." She paused, grinning. "Want to see it? We're not done with all the detail, but it's mostly finished."

"Oh, yes, please!"

In the back, on Allen's large baking table, there was a four-tiered cake, iced with white frosting. As Lillie had indicated, it did have some delicate flowers piped on with light pink icing, and some decor around the edges. It certainly looked like several hours' worth of work.

"Anything, erm, *special* in this?" Bev asked, walking around the table to inspect it.

"We did brush on some lemon simple syrup," Lillie said. "Just to ensure the flavor and—Oh. You mean *special*-special." She barked a laugh. "I wouldn't dream of it with Allen's father roaming around."

"Good," Bev said. "You never know what those soldiers are up to."

Lillie shook her head so hard a stray golden curl fell from her bun. "Allen's been testing everything I make, to be on the safe side. He'd never forgive himself if something happened to anyone because of his father."

"He's a good egg," Bev said. "Has Zed been sniffing around here at all?"

"No, why?"

"I don't think he's being completely honest about why he's in town," Bev said. "I fear he might be looking for Lower Pigsend."

Lillie stopped, the color draining from her face. "No…"

"I can't be sure, of course," Bev said. "But every soldier who came to town said they were looking for something—or someone—powerful," Bev said. "I honestly thought it might've been, well…" Her cheeks warmed. "Me. But now I'm not so sure. They were so keen on destroying everything magical after the war, and I can't imagine the queen would be content until everything was actually wiped off the map."

Lillie bit her lip. "Someone should warn Percival. Maybe he can make the talisman stronger."

"I saw Nog at the farmers' market," Bev said. "And I told him, but it's anyone's guess if he told

Percival about it. I'd go visit Merv, but I don't want to even go in that direction, lest I'm followed."

"Good idea," Lillie said. "Nothing else needs to go wrong this week, I swear. Poor Allen's about to have a nervous breakdown, and I'm surprised Vicky hasn't fainted from stress."

"Well, if Karen has anything to do with it, it hopefully won't," Bev said.

Lillie shook her head. "Are you liking her these days? I thought you suspected her of ruining the wedding."

Bev smiled. "Not anymore. Found out some interesting things about her today."

"Oh?"

"Did Allen tell you where he got Vicky's ring?" Bev asked. "Or anything about a barus?"

"A barus? What in the world is he doing messing with one of those creatures?" She made a face. "Tricksters. Always get you in the first bit, and make you come back for more."

"Yes, we all learned that lesson," Bev said. "Karen found him and got a bit of leprechaun luck."

"Leprechaun." Lillie let out a low whistle. "That might not have been the best idea."

"What do you mean?"

"Well, they'll give you a bit of luck, but there's always a loophole," Lillie said. "At least, that's what my mother told me once upon a time."

"Let's hope that loophole doesn't show up until

the day after the wedding," Bev said.

"Why did she want that anyway?" Lillie asked, lowering her voice to match Karen's intense one. "Surely, if you listen to her, she's an *expert* at weddings."

"Apparently not." Bev told her about Karen skipping out on a wedding, and how she was hoping to make a good impression on Marion.

"So we've ruled out Karen as the culprit," Lillie said. "Who else is on the list?"

Bev let out a breath. "Karen thought Marion was acting a bit dodgy. Zed, too, seems to be in town for some other reason. But honestly, I'm hoping Karen's luck is enough. I can't imagine what else could go wrong."

~

Bev returned to the inn, grateful the front room was empty, save Clarice snoozing with Biscuit at her feet. She had a bit of laundry to get through, some light dusting, and some prep work for her part in the giant feast she'd be responsible for. She assembled ten loaves of bread to be proofed in the root cellar overnight, and triple checked she had all the ingredients for the side dishes.

At a quarter-to-three, Wallace returned and called, "Are you in here, Bev?"

"Yes," Bev called from the kitchen. "What can I do for you?"

"I was hoping to find a space to counsel the

happy couple this afternoon," he said. "Do you have any ideas?"

"You could probably try the bakery," Bev said, nodding toward the front door.

"Ah, I think I want to do it on more neutral ground," he said with a laugh. "I was hoping I could commandeer your kitchen for a bit. Seems private enough, and we won't run the risk of anyone walking through."

"I'll be in there getting dinner ready," Bev said. "But if the couple's happy with that, then—"

Said happy couple walked in, with Marion in tow, arguing in low tones.

Allen muttered, "Need to finish decorating the cake."

"Let Lillie do it. She'll probably be faster than you anyway," Vicky replied tensely.

"But I want to do it. I'm the baker."

"You're also the groom," Vicky retorted. "I daresay that's a *bit* more important than being the town baker."

"Too right," Marion announced.

Vicky and Allen turned, as if they hadn't realized she was behind them. "Aunt Marion," Vicky said, her cheeks turning red. "When did you get here?"

"I guess you two didn't notice as you've been, ahem, *deep* in discussions," she said with a sideways look. "But I understand the cleric would like to offer you counseling, so I wanted to make myself available."

"Why?" Allen snapped.

"Well, to be a neutral third party," Marion said, as if the answer were obvious.

Wallace made a face, but Vicky waved him off. "Fine. She can stay. We need to get this out in the open."

Allen caught Bev's gaze and nodded at her. "Bev, you can stay, too."

"This is supposed to be…" Wallace began but cleared his throat. "Well, if both parties are fine with it, why don't we sit down here in the front room?"

"I'll listen from the kitchen," Bev said, not really wanting to be a part of this.

"Bev, please," Allen said, giving her a look.

"Well, I suppose I can chop vegetables after," Bev said with a sigh as she took a seat next to Wallace.

The cleric opened his book and cleared his throat. "Now, to begin… I want to know more about you two. Where did you meet?"

"Here in town," Vicky said. "Allen and I were in school together. It sort of…happened."

"Not many girls to pick from," Allen said then quickly added, "But I like Vicky the best of them. Or else I wouldn't be marrying her."

Wallace scribbled something in his book. "And how long have you been together?"

"Erm…" Vicky thought for a moment.

"That's a good question," Allen said, sharing a look with her. "From the beginning or from the last time we broke up?"

Wallace smiled, but there was tension there. "Let's say both."

"We first kissed when I was eighteen and you'd turned twenty-two," Vicky said. "And I think we've been together…"

"You broke up with me the night we got engaged," Allen said. "Do we count that?"

"Oh, obviously not," Vicky said with a scowl. "I wasn't serious about that—"

"Weren't you? You chucked bread at my head."

"I was angry because you were keeping secrets again."

"The *secret* was that I was off getting your engagement ring."

"A ring you won't let me wear—"

"Ahem," Wallace cleared his throat, "so it seems like we've had some discord in the relationship. You're twenty, Vicky? And you're almost twenty-four, Allen?"

They nodded.

"And it seems you've been together for two years, on and off?"

Again, they nodded.

"Perhaps it's best to move to a different thread of conversation," Marion said. "I don't think it's wise to dwell on the past."

"Okay." Wallace turned the page. "Let's discuss your vision for your relationship. Are you thinking of starting a family?"

They nodded.

"Excellent," Wallace said, looking relieved. "Are you two on the same page with how many children and when you want to start?"

"Right away," Vicky said at the same time as Allen said, "A few years."

They stared at each other, clearly shocked at the other's response.

"A few *years*?" Vicky said. "Allen, I don't want to wait a few *years*. We're married. Why not start now?"

"We've gone into debt paying for this wedding, that's why," Allen said. "We need to get ourselves settled before we add any more chaos to our lives."

"Children aren't *chaos*," Vicky said with narrowed eyes.

"Aren't they?" Marion muttered to herself.

"Look, I want a family. But not now. I'm not saying never, but we're so young. There's no rush," Allen said. "Besides that, we'll probably have Grant to take care of for the next few years until he finds himself a job, and goodness knows when *that* will be."

Vicky turned to him, color in her cheeks. "My brother is *not* up for discussion. You know that."

"I know he's skipped town instead of staying here to help you," Allen shot back. "I know I've bent over backward trying to get him a job with everyone—Bev included—and he's decided they aren't for him every time. The boy needs to learn how to work, or else—"

"Or else what? We'll be stuck paying for him?" Vicky said. "He'll figure it out. But he's not... He told Bev he skipped town because he thought he was cursed."

Bev, who'd hoped to blend into the background, winced.

"I think we're getting off track again," Wallace said, holding up his hands. "Let's get to some basic questions, then maybe we'll take a break and come back to these other topics tomorrow." He flipped his book again. "Allen, what do you appreciate the most about Vicky?"

He opened his mouth, but nothing came out for a moment. "Erm. I'm not sure."

"Allen." Vicky rolled her eyes.

"Vicky, same question to you," Wallace said, almost as a dare.

"Well, erm..." Her cheeks turned pink again. "Allen is...well, he's..." She stammered, much to the smug relief of her fiancé.

"What do you value about the relationship?" Wallace said, clearly trying again. "Why are you together? Why do you want to get married?"

"Because we love each other," Allen said, this time without hesitation. "And she told me if I didn't marry her, she'd leave me, so—"

"That's not a reason," Vicky snapped.

"Well, it's true, isn't it?" Allen said. "I didn't want to lose you, so I did what you asked. I've paid for everything you wanted in this wedding. I've broken my back making cakes and cookies and pies and tarts and whatever else anyone's asked of me so you can have the dream wedding you always wanted. And I'm sorry if I'm not more verbal about what you mean to me, but the truth is, I'm exhausted and ready for this stupid thing to be over with."

"We're both working hard," Vicky said, softly. "And I do see it and appreciate it."

"That's more like it," Wallace said. "You two were scaring me there for a bit. I was about to advise that you *don't* get married—"

"Well, perhaps you should," Marion said, her voice icy.

Vicky and Allen turned to stare at her. She'd been uncharacteristically quiet during their back-and-forth, but now it seemed she was ready to say her piece.

"Victoria, one of my biggest regrets in life is not convincing your mother to make a different decision," Marion said with a slow shake of her head. "Not that I think I could've changed her mind, but I wish I'd tried harder. I don't know if you ever knew this, but your mother was betrothed to another man. A very wealthy man in Sheepsburg. It had been planned for years."

Vicky nodded. "She told me she hated him. Met my father and saw her way out."

"Yes, well." Marion shifted. "It certainly caused more than a little consternation. Our families had been very close, and when your mother broke off the engagement, it caused a rift that was never mended. She was *so sure* marrying your father was the right thing, she had no care for the damage it caused the rest of us. And what did it get her—"

"Two beautiful children and a lifetime of happiness," Vicky ground out between gritted teeth.

"Well, if you can call what she had a *lifetime*," Marion said, waving her hand absentmindedly. "And your father, leaving you two in the lurch like that. But you know, it all comes down to stock. Marry the right person, and you'll never have to worry. But the wrong person…"

"I think you'll find, as soon as you get to know Allen, that I'm making the right decision," Vicky said, her cheeks turning red. "And *thank you* for your concern. It was perfectly articulated to me in the several letters you sent after our wedding announcement."

"Which I think is rich considering you've never lifted a finger to help Vicky or Grant," Allen said.

"You don't know her, you don't know me, and you don't know anything about our relationship."

"From what I've heard now, I think I know *plenty*," Marion said. "I'm saying…going into a marriage because it's the only taste of love is a recipe for heartache. I wish you could spread your wings, see the world, go somewhere other than this small town—"

"I think we're getting off track again," Wallace said, his gaze on the affianced couple. "Ms. Bilensbrook, your concerns are duly noted. But I think it's best if I'm the one guiding the conversation. I've had plenty of experience with these kinds of things and—"

The door burst open and Lillie ran in, her eyes wide and her hair flying around her face.

"Allen! Come quick! It's…the cake!"

CHAPTER SEVENTEEN

"I can't believe it," Allen said, his eyes wide. "How did *one of the table legs fall off*?"

Bev couldn't believe it either. The cake had been sitting atop his kitchen table, which was now half on the floor as one leg seemed to have shattered. One delicately-piped flower was still pristine, but the rest was a mess of sponge and sugar. It was a complete disaster.

"Was the cake too heavy?" Wallace asked, keeping a steady hand on Vicky, who was whimpering softly.

"It shouldn't have been," Allen said, looking far more upset than his bride. "It was a sturdy table. My mom's table." He looked up at Lillie, pleading in his gaze. "What happened?"

"I-I have no idea," Lillie said, her voice trembling and face pale. "I wasn't even *in* here. I was out f-front. There was a c-customer." She looked at Bev. "Then I heard this loud crash and came back and…" She gestured to the mess on the floor. "Oh, Allen. I'm so sorry. This is devastating."

"Can't you make another one?" Vicky asked, her voice quiet.

"This one took us days," Allen said, rubbing his face. "Pounds and pounds of flour and sugar and…" He groaned as he covered his eyes. "How did this *happen*?"

Bev knelt to inspect the table, searching for any signs of weakness. She found a screw on the ground and picked it up, inspecting it.

Allen took it and barked a laugh of surprise. "Of course it did. Of *course*. Why wouldn't a screw fall out of my table instead of staying in and holding up the cake I spent *hours* painstakingly decorating—"

"How does a screw fall out of a table?" Bev asked, looking around.

"Well, are we *sure* it fell out?" Marion asked, giving Lillie a once-over. "Maybe this *woman* is responsible for causing all this chaos?"

"Me?" Lillie blanched. "Why me? I was in the other room—"

"I can see it now," Marion continued. "Long nights in the bakery, a jealousy arose. You decided to loosen the screw in the table, enough that it would become unsteady, until—"

"I've only worked here a month," Lillie snapped, glaring at Marion. "And Allen *and* Vicky have been nothing but kind to me. I would *never* do anything to hurt either of them. Not after all they've done for me."

"It wasn't Lillie," Allen said with a low sigh. "Two weeks ago, I asked Earl to strip and reseal the table. It was getting a bit worn, with all the work I'd been doing, and I wanted to make sure it would hold up. I guess he forgot to tighten this one, or maybe it wasn't in right, but…"

Allen groaned and tipped forward, and if it wasn't for Lillie grabbing him by the shoulder, he would've gone straight into the icing.

Vicky swallowed, for once not looking the most upset. "Allen, maybe we don't need a big cake—"

"Yes, we do," Allen said, kneeling to pick up the pieces. "Is any of this salvageable?"

It certainly didn't look like it was. But as the moments ticked on, the shock left Lillie's face and was replaced by determination. "I can salvage it."

Bev knew what she was thinking and sat. "Lillie, are you sure—"

"It'll be fine," Lillie snapped. "Allen, you and Vicky don't worry one bit. There *will* be a cake at your wedding. I promise." She stood and dusted her hands off. "Now, first thing, I need every one of those pans cleaned, buttered, and floured. Then I need to remake the sponges..." She slapped her head. "I need more flour. Lots of it. Is the miller still open?"

"I can catch him if I hurry," Bev said. "I'll leave now."

"Here, Bev—" Allen said, reaching into his pocket.

Bev waved him off. "I've got this. You two get to cleaning. We have a cake to make!"

~

Bev rushed across the street, bypassing the inn completely to get Sin hooked up to the wagon and on the road. She worried, of course, about Lillie's plan. Bev had no doubts the pobyd would be able to recreate the cake, perhaps not exactly like Allen had envisioned, but it would be gorgeous, nonetheless. Bev's concern was the sparkle in Lillie's eye that said she was planning to use magic to help the process along.

"Oh, Lillie, please don't get yourself in trouble," Bev muttered, tightening the straps on Sin.

Bev set off, goading Sin as fast as the old mule would go.

It was getting on in the afternoon, and Sonny would be closing up shop at sundown. Bev hoped he had a mill full of flour to sell, but she was starting to worry that the charm Karen got hadn't worked. What else could explain the continued string of bad luck?

Speaking of Karen, as the main road emptied in the town square, the event planner had finished setting up all the tables and chairs and was hanging beautiful green garlands over the tent entrance.

"What is it?" Karen asked as Bev came running over.

"You might want to turn that charm on," Bev said.

Karen's eyes widened. "Why?"

Bev told her about the faulty table leg, and Karen let out an uncharacteristically whiny moan.

"You have *got* to be kidding me." She pulled out the bauble from her pocket and inspected it. "I swear the barus gave me the right thing. It feels lucky. Why isn't it working?"

"I don't know," Bev said.

"Well, it *should* be obvious." Etheldra stood on the other side of the road, looking like she'd closed up at the tea shop.

"I'm sorry?" Karen said with a look.

"I said, it *should* be obvious what's going on. Bev, surprised you haven't solved it yet."

Bev opened and closed her mouth, not understanding what Etheldra was saying.

"Goodness, have to do *everything* around here." Without another word, she crossed the street, climbed into the wagon, and looked ahead. When nobody moved, she barked, "What are you gawking at me for? Don't you have a wedding to save, girl? Get to the bakery and find out what in the world happened!"

Karen jumped, realizing she was the one being addressed, then scampered off toward the bakery.

"W-what are you doing?" Bev asked.

"Helping you, clearly," Etheldra drawled. "Since you haven't a clue what you're doing." She made a noise. "Onward, mule!"

Sin brayed, clearly annoyed at being spoken to by anyone other than Bev.

"Don't you take that tone with me," Etheldra brayed back.

"Sin, let's go," Bev said, tapping her on the rump. "What do you mean, you're helping me?"

"I told you two days ago you have a curse," Etheldra said. "Clearly, you haven't done much about it, eh?"

"I mean…" Bev started. "You weren't serious about that, were you? A—"

"A curse. As in someone cast a spell on Vicky or the wedding or what have you," Etheldra continued. "And bad things will continue to happen until you break that curse."

Bev stared at her. "How am I supposed to break a curse?"

"Well, I don't know," she said, eyeing Bev. "Don't you have people who know about those things?"

Bev swallowed. She *did*, but she wasn't keen on going to see him at the moment. "Karen got a bit of luck," Bev said. "The magical kind. We thought—"

"You need more than *luck* to break a curse. Doesn't anyone know anything around here?" Etheldra huffed. "You need an honest-to-goodness counterspell. Or you need to find out who's cursed the wedding and get *them* to break it."

That somehow seemed harder. "I don't know who's interested in cursing the wedding," Bev said.

"You've got an inn full of suspects, haven't you?"

"It's not always someone at the inn," Bev said.

"Isn't it, though?"

"No, the—" Bev stopped herself before she revealed PJ's real nature. "*Anyway.*"

"Stop here," Etheldra said.

"Why?"

"Because my house is right there, and I plan on telling Earl to stop by the bakery to fix that wobbly table," she replied, pulling on the reins to slow the mule. "I suppose I'll be seeing you for dinner in a few hours. Don't be thinking you can skimp out on dinner, or worse yet, serve *barley soup*. I expect a full spread and rosemary bread, and don't let me catch you doing anything less."

With that, Etheldra disappeared between two houses and was gone.

⌣

Bev managed to get to the miller's and—as luck

would have it—he did have several pounds of flour. Bev heaved a sigh of relief as she headed back toward the bakery. That was, until she glanced upward at the sky.

"Don't you *dare*," she muttered.

The clouds had certainly turned darker, and the smell of rain was heavy in the air. Bev goaded Sin on faster, wishing she'd had the foresight to bring something to cover the bags. The mule, predictably, did not walk with any extra speed, and Bev's heart began thumping as a big splotch of rain hit her nose.

"Come on, Sin," Bev said. "You know you don't like to be wet. If you don't hurry, you won't get back to the stable before—"

The sky opened and rain pelted Bev, Sin, and the flour in the wagon. Bev let out a sigh of frustration, but at least Sin finally got the message and picked up her speed. There was nothing to be done about the flour now, and Bev had to hope that the covers they were in would offer some protection, or that she'd gotten enough that the wet flour wouldn't cause a problem. But the rain was hitting so hard it was getting difficult to see, and Bev's hopes sank.

She wasn't even at the bakery before the front door opened, and Allen and Karen ran out.

"Hurry!" Bev said, jumping off as fast as she could. There were five bags of flour in the back of the wagon. Allen took two, Bev took two, and Karen took one as they dashed inside the bakery. The table had been haphazardly repaired, but it still shook as twenty-five pounds of flour were set down on it. Bev huffed and puffed as she wiped the rain off her face. Thankfully, Vicky was gone, as were Marion and Wallace, so it was the four of them, dripping and staring at the soaking wet flour.

"I tried to rush," Bev said. "I'm so sorry, Allen."

"I'm sure it's all right," Allen said, though he sounded dubious. As he opened the first bag, he pulled out a wet clump of flour and let out a breath. "Oh, me. It's all ruined."

"It's not," Lillie said, giving Bev a look. "I can handle this."

"Lillie, I appreciate your optimism," Karen said. "But—"

"I'm a pobyd," Lillie said quietly, looking at Karen with a sideways glance.

"A pob…" Karen cleared her throat, her gaze turning to the golden-haired woman. "I thought you were all gone?"

"Not quite," Lillie said softly, kneeling by the bags.

"Are you sure you want to do this?" Bev asked. "Won't the magic be detectable?"

"Perhaps," she said softly. "If someone really wanted to find it, they probably could."

"We can maybe dry it in the oven," Allen said.

"Spread it out on baking sheets, and—"

"Look, I made my bed," Lillie cut him off. "I'm the one who got myself kicked out of Lower Pigsend. So if I get hauled away in handcuffs, it's my own fault. I'm going to use magic to dry this flour, and I'm going to use magic to make your wedding cake. And that's that."

She sounded so firm that it was hard for Bev to argue. "If you insist."

"That's settled then," Lillie said, placing her hands on the bags. The room filled with the scent of spice and sweet, and the bags changed colors before Bev's eyes. "There. All fixed."

"Lillie, we're certainly grateful you're here," Allen said, placing a hand on her shoulder. "I—"

"I heard the cake fell over?"

Everyone's expressions melted into ones of fear as Zed walked into the room. He was soaking wet from the rain, but he still wore that casual smile.

"Y-yeah," Karen said, after a long pause. "Another freak accident."

"Been having a lot of those, haven't we?" Zed said, looking between the four others in the room. "Bad luck and good marriages, eh?"

"You said it," Bev said.

"And this rain! It came out of nowhere, didn't it?" He put his hands in his pockets. "I'm soaked through and through. Bev, you look like you got caught out in it. Your mule was looking right put out to be there."

"Shoot." Bev put her hand to her head. "Sin is going to be furious."

"I got her back to the stable," he said with a laugh. "Saw you coming down the road and when I didn't see you come back out immediately, I got her all set. I think she might've remembered me, you know. Didn't take my fingers off, as I half-expected her to."

Bev said a small prayer of thanks that Sin had behaved.

But her heart sank when Zed's gaze fell to the flour on the ground. Had he seen how sopping wet the flour bags were when they'd brought them inside? "They're…dry?"

"I had a good cover on them," Bev said, almost a little too quickly. "Luckily, I looked at the sky before I left. We had to hurry, but we got them all inside."

Zed walked to the large bin in the corner, where the first version of Allen's cake had been swept up and thrown away. He dipped his finger into the icing and sponge mixture sticking out the top and took a bite. "Well, that is a shame. It's delicious, Allen. You really did your mother proud." He turned to Allen with a warm smile on his face. "I only wish she was here to see you. But it seems she sent you Lillie to help."

"And we're so glad she did," Allen said.

"Well, the day is wearing on," Karen said,

seeming to snap out of the shock before anyone else. "Lillie, dear, you said you needed space. So why don't we head across the street? Bev, I'm sure you could dry off a bit and get going on dinner, eh?"

"You know, it's been a few years, but I'm sure I remember how to work an oven," Zed said. "Let me help you—"

"No!" Allen, Bev, and Lillie said in unison.

"Well, I promise I won't ruin anything!" Zed said with a hearty laugh. "Maybe I can help rebuild the table, or—"

"Etheldra's sending Earl to help," said Bev, who'd almost forgotten her conversation with the tea shop owner. "I'm sure he'll be by any minute."

"Oh, good," Allen said.

"Right, because I do need a table to work on," Lillie said with a nervous laugh that made Bev think the pobyd *didn't* need a table.

The group stared at each other, the tension growing thick again.

"Karen's right," Bev said with a loud clearing of her throat. "We do have to be getting on with things. Why don't we all head back to the inn, and I'll put on a kettle for everyone? I've got to bring Sin some carrots, too, else she'll probably never do anything for me again." She turned to Allen. "Allen, I don't think you've had a chance to catch up with your father, have you?"

"Er, no, but—"

"Perhaps now's a good time," Bev said, with a pointed look. If Allen was with Zed, the soldier wouldn't be in the bakery and wouldn't see Lillie using magic.

"Surely, Lillie needs help in here," Zed said with a frown.

"I work better alone," Lillie replied with a tight smile. "Besides, they've got me all set with the sponge pans. Just need to start getting them in the oven. Nothing I can't handle." She gestured to Allen. "Go have a cup of tea with your father."

Chapter Eighteen

The rain was coming down hard, and even the short distance between the bakery and the inn was enough to soak the entire group. Bev fetched some extra blankets from her storage rooms to help everyone mop up, before heading out to check on Sin. The mule was quite grouchy and nearly took off Bev's fingers when offered a carrot.

"Hey, don't blame me," Bev said. "You're the one who took her time walking."

When Bev returned to the inn, she once again mopped the rain off herself and checked on dinner. That, at least, was going swimmingly, with a beautiful roast beef coupled with her herbs and a bit of the wine Lillie had fixed. The bread, too, was ready for the oven, so Bev popped them in before heading out to check on her guests in the front room.

Someone had started a fire, which was welcome after the deluge. Marion and Clarice sat in two armchairs, the former reading and the latter snoozing with a smile. Bev couldn't help but notice Marion's gaze drifting to Allen, but thankfully, the baker's ire seemed to be focused on his father.

Allen faced his father, an open bottle of Lillie's addled wine between them and two full glasses sitting untouched. Zed, to his credit, looked a little uncomfortable, while Allen glowered at his father with all the pent-up hate of eight years of no contact.

"So…" Zed began. "Some weather we're having, eh?"

"Seems right, considering," Allen replied.

"Well, you know what they say—"

"Don't you dare say it," Allen snapped. "If one more person says bad luck makes a good marriage, I'm going to scream."

Zed cleared his throat. "Well, the cake certainly tasted delicious. I'm sure the one at the wedding will be as good. You've become quite the baker!"

Allen let out a snort.

"The pastries in the morning are delicious."

"Lillie's been making them," Allen retorted. "As I have to take our deliveries."

"Yes, you've been doing some business this week. I don't remember your mother ever being so busy."

"Have a wedding to pay for." He glared at Marion. "Since no one else is going to put up any money. Why are you even here, if you're so opposed to our marriage?"

"I'm here to support my niece," Marion replied. "Where has she run off to?"

"Home, I'd wager," Allen snapped. "Probably crying her eyes out yet again. Who cries that much before their wedding?"

"Well, I think it proves my point, then, doesn't it?" Marion replied with a sideways look.

"What point?" Zed asked.

Before Marion could answer, Karen rushed in, her cloak dripping as she shook it off and hung it on a peg by the door. She wiped the water from her face, rushing over to the fireplace to warm up before addressing the crowd.

"Well, the tent is holding for now," Karen said, brushing the water off her shoulders. "I'm sure this weather will move on. It's raining so hard. It can't last very long."

Bev didn't want to think about it. "Well, in any case, there will be a beef roast for supper, so that should warm everyone right up. It'll be done soon, along with the bread and wine and…"

She was hoping the prospect of dinner would

lighten things up, but everyone continued to glower in silence.

A few minutes before six, Earl and Etheldra arrived, placing their sopping wet cloaks next to Karen's. Etheldra made a comment about Bardoff not wanting to walk in the rain, and how soft the schoolteacher was, but Earl went right up to Allen and took his hand.

"Tell me it isn't true," he said, his eyes wide with horror. "I swear, every screw in that table was tightened."

"It's all right, Earl," Allen said, though Bev knew it certainly wasn't. "Things happen."

"Not to me," he said. "Let me pop over there and—"

"Not right now," Allen said, a little hastily. "Erm, Lillie needed space to get everything put together. I'll head back over after dinner, and we can get that table put back together for her."

"Can't believe you're letting her do all that work by herself," Zed said with a shake of his head. "I really can help—"

"She's got it handled," Allen said firmly.

"I'm going to bring her dinner," Bev said, picking up the extra bowl. She didn't want Allen to do it, in case Zed followed him across the street. "Be back in a moment." She paused, glancing at Allen, Zed, and Marion. "Everyone behave until I get back."

Bev was sure to rap loudly on the door and announce herself, even if it meant a few extra moments getting rained on. She opened the door and found Lillie standing in the middle of the kitchen, whisking and humming to herself. Four more bowls sat on the ground, spinning of their own volition, the mixture sloshing around as if some invisible force were moving it.

Bev hadn't really seen Lillie's magic in action before, but found herself mesmerized by the bowls turning by themselves, the ingredients inside mixing together. The oven already held several sponge pans, and more sat ready to receive the mix.

"Lillie?" Bev said again.

She jumped but, luckily, all the bowls stopped moving. She turned, her hand on her heart as she inhaled. "Oh, Bev. You gave me a fright."

"I knocked, but I guess you didn't hear me," Bev said, closing the door behind her. "Goodness knows it's loud enough out there."

"Still coming down, eh?" Lillie said. "Hope that tent is sturdy."

"Karen said it was holding," Bev said. "I don't want to think about it." She lifted the bowl in her hand. "Thought I'd bring you something to eat. I know you're going to be working into the night."

"You said it," Lillie said with a sigh. "I'll be happy if I can get all the sponges baked tonight.

There's fifteen of them, you know. Five tiers with three layers each. I've got the first set in the oven now, and I'm working on round two. They take about half an hour each, but there's so many, I can only do a couple at a time." She sighed with a smile. "The icing is what takes the longest. All the piping, all the detail. I do love a challenge, but goodness me, this is going to be a big one."

One of the bowls stopped spinning, and Lillie put down the one she was holding to inspect it. As soon as the one in her arms touched the ground, it spun, as the others were.

"How are you doing that?" Bev asked, nodding to the three bowls rotating.

"I can't levitate or anything like that," Lillie said. "But my magic can make the flour move in the bowl, make the egg whisk itself, that sort of thing. Saves a little bit of time, you know? And I need all the help I can get."

"Can I do anything for you?" Bev asked.

Lillie shoveled a large spoonful of dinner into her mouth. "Oh, Bef. Fis ish amashing!" She swallowed. "You outdid yourself tonight."

"You say that every night." Bev gave her a sideways look.

"It's been a few nights since I've had your cooking," Lillie said with a cheeky smile. "My dinners have been bread and cheese with a bit of fruit as of late. Not the worst, but not roast beef."

Bit of fruit? Bev didn't want to pry about where Lillie was taking the baskets of produce she'd been buying at the market. Instead, she walked over to the table, which had been pushed to the side to make room for all of Lillie's bowls. "Poor Earl is beside himself across the street. Blames himself."

"I don't think it was Earl," Lillie said, pushing her spoon into the meat.

"What?"

"Bev, I have to be honest," Lillie said. "I think this wedding is cursed."

"That's what Etheldra said," Bev replied.

"There's no other explanation," Lillie said. "No one was in here. I swear it. And Vicky's dress and the wine and…" She sighed. "It's too much to be coincidence."

"I agree," Bev said. "But I haven't a clue what to do about it."

Lillie licked her lips. "Ask Percival."

"Percival?" Bev frowned. "I couldn't… Not with Zed staying at the inn. What if he follows me?"

"Then have someone keep tabs on him to make sure he doesn't," Lillie said. "Biscuit or whomever. Unless someone figures out what's going on, things are going to keep happening. And yes, you can have a wedding without a cake or a dress or any of that, but I daresay the bride's about to keel over from stress."

"And Allen, too," Bev said. She paused, looking

around. "Lillie, I'm worried about them."

"Me, too. He's been so grumpy—"

"Not because of that." She told Lillie about the counseling session that had come to an abrupt halt at the cake news.

Lillie listened and shook her head. "I'm no expert in relationships, least of all theirs. But it does seem they've sort of…lost the plot a bit. This is supposed to be a happy occasion. And yes, there have been a lot of mishaps, and perhaps it's their nature to let things get to them, but…" She sighed. "I don't know. I'm baking the cake."

Bev nodded. "I'd probably better get back over there. Marion, Allen, and Zed were about to get into it, and goodness knows we don't need them fighting." She nodded to the broken table. "Earl did mention he wanted to get back over here and fix the table. Do you think you could put a pin in the magic for a bit so he could do that?"

"Send him over," Lillie said, leaning against the counter with the bowl cupped between her hands. "I've got to wait for these sponges to get out anyway, so I've got a few minutes."

Bev hesitated, her hand near the doorknob. "If I'm going to see about breaking this curse, I've got to get to Percival tomorrow. So it appears I'll be heading to Merv's in the morning. Do you…" She paused. "Is there anything you want me to bring?"

Lillie's face softened. "I may be able to spare a

few wedding cookies. If you feel like taking them to him, I'd love to know what he thinks." She beamed. "I'll have them with the breakfast pastries in the morning."

When Bev returned to the inn, she was met by loud, raised voices. Allen and Zed stood on one side of the inn, glaring at Marion, Vicky, Lucy, and Nadia on the other. Wallace stood somewhat between them. Paul was reading a book in the corner and looking uninterested. Clarice held Biscuit in her lap, watching the volleys with concern.

"You've done nothing but look down your nose at us," Allen snapped, pointing his finger at Marion. "And frankly, I'm sick of hearing your voice—"

"Allen, don't yell at my aunt," Vicky shot back at him. "She's come all this way to celebrate our wedding, and you've done absolutely nothing but avoid her—"

"I'm not *avoiding* anything!" Allen cried. "I'm working my fingers to the bone to pay for this wedding so *you* can impress *her!*" He gestured toward Marion. "And for what? So you can have one day where you're better than your aunts?"

"It's supposed to be the best day of our lives," Vicky shot back, her face red. "And it's not to impress anyone—"

"Isn't it? All I've heard for the past few weeks is

how important it is, and how *this* wedding must be better than *that* wedding you attended in Sheepsburg," Allen continued. "Then she gets here, and everything's wrong!" He waved his hand toward Lucy. "Lucy's the only one who seems genuinely interested in your well-being."

"I care!" Marion huffed. "I gave you that bracelet."

Vicky ran her fingers along the gems. "Yeah, she gave me this bracelet."

"A bracelet," Allen scoffed. "You're happy to give her that, but not three hours ago, you said we shouldn't get married?"

"You said *what*?" Zed turned to her, shocked. "Why would you say such a thing?"

"Come now, Zed, you have to agree," Marion said, gesturing toward the couple. "They've done nothing but argue and—"

"And Fernley and I did the same," Zed said with a wave of his hand.

"Not exactly a vote of confidence," Allen muttered.

"May I interject here?" Wallace said, stepping forward.

"No, you may not," Marion replied. "I think you've done enough with your ridiculous attempt at counseling earlier—"

"Ridiculous?" Wallace's brows rose. "I'll have you know, *madam*, that I've counseled hundreds of couples on their wedding days, and many of them went on to have long, fruitful, *happy* marriages—"

"Clearly, you're doing wonders here," Marion said, gesturing to Vicky and Allen.

"Seems you've lost your touch since you lost your ring, dear," Paul muttered from the corner.

"I think it's clear that this couple is neither happy nor well-suited for one another," Marion said. "Vicky, you really should reconsider—"

Bev put her fingers to her lips and blew, letting out a loud whistle that got everyone's attention. Marion's nostrils flared at the imposition, but the squabbling, at least, stopped for the moment.

"Everybody take a *breath*," Bev said, putting up her hands. "Goodness me, this is not how we act in my inn, understand?" She waited for them to argue, and when they didn't, she put her hands on her hips and continued. "I know tensions are high right now," Bev said. "But I'm not going to have an all-out brawl at my inn. We're having a wedding tomorrow. And that's supposed to be *happy*, remember?"

Allen ducked his head, and Vicky sniffed back tears. Zed was chastened, Lucy stared at the floor, Nadia looked bored, and Marion heaved a loud breath.

"I think it's time everyone heads to bed," Bev said. "Cool down, get some rest. It's going to be a long day tomorrow."

She glared daggers at everyone, waiting for the first person to move.

Earl cleared his throat loudly. "Is, erm, Lillie able to let me pop over and—"

Bev nodded, thumbing at the door. Earl pulled on his cap and dashed out without another word.

"Suppose I'd better go, too," Etheldra said, rising with a knowing look at Bev. "Told you I think this wedding is cursed. Cursed, cursed, cursed."

"Thank you for that vote of confidence," Allen said.

"Not your fault, dear," Etheldra said, patting him on the shoulder. "*Someone* needs to get her act together and solve the problem."

Bev scowled but didn't respond.

"I think I'll head upstairs, too," Clarice said. "Ms. Lucy, will you—"

"Of course." Lucy took her arm and helped her up the stairs.

"Nadia," Marion said. "We *do* have a long day tomorrow. Must get our beauty rest."

They, too, ascended the stairs.

"Come, Vicky, I'll walk you home," Karen said, eyeing Allen with more than a little malice. "After all, it's bad luck to see your groom before your wedding, isn't it?"

"Might be a change of pace to actually invite bad luck instead of stumble on it," Vicky grumbled, pulling on her cloak before setting off in the pouring rain.

Then it was Allen, Zed, and Bev.

"I've got to go check on Lillie," Allen grumbled, walking out the door and slamming it behind him.

"Well, I can certainly say that's not how it was the night before our wedding," Zed said, looking at Bev. "What in the world's gotten into everyone?"

"I don't know," Bev said, a plan forming in her mind. "But I'm surely going to find out."

As soon as she asked a wizard how to un-curse a wedding.

Chapter Nineteen

The day of Allen and Vicky's wedding dawned as stormy and dark as the night before. Under normal circumstances, Bev would've waited until better weather to make the trek to Merv's. Not to mention, the wedding was set to begin at four in the afternoon, and Bev's list of things to do was already overflowing without an impromptu trip. But it was clear that she needed answers, and she could only imagine what else could go wrong if she waited too long.

Well before dawn, Lillie arrived with a basket of breakfast biscuits—flour discs with bacon and cheese usually reserved for emergencies.

"How's it going?" Bev asked the pobyd, who

looked about dead on her feet. "Surprised you could spare a few moments to bake these."

"Oh, Allen made them," Lillie said with a yawn. She certainly looked like she hadn't gotten any sleep. "I'm taking a quick break to deliver them. Allen told me to. Said he wanted to take over icing for a bit."

"Did either of you sleep?" Bev asked.

"I caught a nap around three," Lillie said. "Told Allen to go to sleep around midnight. After all, he's the groom. Can't be falling asleep during his vows." She let out another yawn. "But he came back at five to make the biscuits."

"Do you think the cake will be done?" Bev asked.

"It won't be the best thing I've ever done," Lillie said. "But it'll be delicious. And it'll be finished. That's what's most important."

Bev smiled, peering into the basket. Besides the breakfast biscuits, there were a few wrapped items inside. "Are those for...?"

Lillie nodded, pulling them out and handing them to Bev. "Made with a little extra love, if you get my meaning. Do tell him I said hi."

"Perhaps it's time you tell him yourself," Bev said, gently. "I know he misses you."

"After the wedding." Lillie let out another yawn. "Goodness, I've got to get some tea in me and get back to it. All this rain is making things harder."

She opened the front door, pulled her cloak tighter around her shoulders, and threw the still-wet hood over her head then dashed across the street to the bakery.

Bev winced, imagining how drenched she'd be by the time she got to Merv's tunnel. But there was nothing else to be done. Allen and Vicky's wedding depended on her figuring out what was going on.

After setting the biscuits on the center table with a card saying she'd be back later, Bev sighed as she donned her cloak and walking boots. Biscuit, who'd been watching her curiously, whimpered as she went for the kitchen door.

"Don't worry, you're not coming," she replied. "Unless you want to walk through the rain…?"

He promptly sat.

"Figured as much." She pulled her cloak tighter. "You keep an eye on things, yeah? Especially Zed. I've got to get some answers. Before it's too late."

Bev knew the long walk to Merv's home by heart, especially after going every day for nearly a week the month before. She was grateful the chaos down below had ended and everyone was safe. Other than a quick visit to deliver Lillie's apology letter, Bev hadn't been back, and she was looking forward to seeing Merv again, even if it was under dire circumstances.

It took only seconds for the rain to soak her

thoroughly, and even her thick cloak did little to dispel the chill. Still, after a few minutes, she got used to it, and carried on with that stoic determination Wim McKee had taught her.

She passed by the town square and was relieved to see the white tent still somewhat standing. It was leaning to one side a tad, and there were pools of water collecting in pockets, but nothing Karen couldn't fix, probably. Underneath looked to be completely dry, and Bev had to remind herself the town hall itself would be used for the ceremony, so that would presumably be dry.

Unless the roof sprang a leak. Which…was possible, under the circumstances.

Her plan was to say a quick hello and goodbye to Merv then continue on to Lower Pigsend. There, she'd seek out Percival, ask him what he knew about curses, and hope against hope he had some easy fix. Perhaps a more potent talisman, or a spell he could cast… Bev knew very little of how magic worked, but Percival, once restored to his full magical strength, seemed quite learned in the ways magic could be used.

And besides that, she wasn't sure what she'd do if he *wasn't* able to help.

It was still quite early when Bev walked up to the large orange door and rapped loudly, so she couldn't be sure that Merv was even awake. But not a few moments after she'd knocked, the door swung open and the moleman—six foot tall, covered in black fur with long talons—let out a cheer of happiness.

"Bev! You're a sight." He stepped back. "Come in, come in. Get that sopping wet cloak off you and by the fireplace to warm up. Yes, nasty weather you're having up there, aren't you?"

"It's good to see you, Merv," Bev said, taking his invitation to warm herself, if only for a moment. "I need a bit of help. Do you know anything about curses?"

"Curses?" He shook his head. "Not a thing. But I'm sure Percival will be along in a minute, so he can answer that for you?"

"He will?" Bev had assumed she'd have to continue to Lower Pigsend. The door was still visible to her, meaning she was still able to cross over into the town. "How does he know I'm here?"

He chuckled. "Well, after the fiasco with Lillie, I think he's keeping a closer eye on my living room and when I get visitors. Seems to want to check in every time anyone sits down on my couch these days."

"Are you getting many visitors?" Bev asked, a little curiously. The moleman had seemed quite solitary, and with Lillie gone to the upper world, Bev didn't know who else would be calling on him.

He beamed and didn't answer. "Let me see about that tea. I'm sure Percival will be here any minute now."

Bev took her place on the couch and looked around. During the scare a few weeks ago, Merv had knitted up a storm, creating blanket after blanket that had to have no home. Now, however, it seemed there were fewer knitted projects lying about.

"Merv," Bev called. "Where did all your fabric arts go?"

"That's what I wanted to chat with you about! I've started selling them." He beamed at her from the kitchen. "Did you bring anything delectable, or should I wrestle up some dried-out scones?"

Bev cleared her throat. "Lillie actually made some cookies. They're Fernley's recipe. Supposed to be made for the wedding to give the couple good luck."

Merv poked his head out. "Oh, she did? I've already got a dozen of her last batch I'm still working on."

Bev frowned. "Cookies from a month ago?"

"No." Merv stood in the doorframe between the living room and kitchen. "She dropped them off last week."

"She didn't mention you two were talking," Bev said, a little concerned that Lillie was still lying to her.

"We're not exactly talking, no." He returned to the kitchen but kept talking. "A week after she was banished from Lower Pigsend, I heard movement outside my door. Half-expected to see you again, but instead there was a box of warm cookies, a sack of gold coins, and a large crate of fruit."

That certainly explained the fruit. "Why do you think she's doing that?"

"Percival thinks she's trying to make amends," Merv said. "That's how I knew about the charm. He said he was alerted to Lillie's presence, even outside my door. But as I said, she hasn't wanted to come inside for a cup of tea. I'm not sure *she's* ready to face me yet, to be honest."

"Probably not," Bev said. "What do you do with the supplies?"

"I send them along with Percival," he said. "The gold helps them pay that merchant man, and the fruit, obviously, is well received. I understand they're starting to bring in more goods, but…" He sighed.

Bev had seen Nog a few times, but there were so many creatures in Lower Pigsend. "Suppose she's trying to help fill the gap."

"It's not enough to feed an entire village, but it's a start." Percival the wizard strode through the door to Lower Pigsend. He had a long white beard and purple robes and was wearing Bev's old amulet around his neck. Although it had been a few weeks since Bev had seen him, he still looked as healthy and sprightly as before. "Bev, it's lovely to see you again."

"Ah, that'll be the tea," Merv said, as a whistle

echoed from the kitchen.

Percival sat on the chair opposite Bev and beamed at her. "How are things in the upper world?"

"Well, actually, that's why I came to visit Merv," Bev said. "A young couple in town are getting married—"

"Oh, who?" Merv asked. "Allen?

Bev nodded. "And Vicky. But there's a problem. Lots of problems, in fact." Bev told them about all the mishaps occurring in town, and how she was starting to suspect there was a magical reason behind it. "Especially the dress. What kind of bad luck would put the dress at the right angle to catch on fire? Or the table randomly falling down?"

Percival nodded, rubbing his long beard. "It certainly sounds like a curse."

"What can be done?" Bev said, holding her breath.

He clicked his tongue. "They're tricky things because you have to know what was cursed in order to figure out how to break it. For example, if someone cast it on the wedding itself, you'd have to find the caster to undo the spell."

Bev's hopes sank. "Oh, no."

"But that would certainly take a magical expert of extraordinary ability, especially if the caster isn't nearby," Percival said. "If you were to ask *me* to curse the wedding from down here, I don't know if

I'd be able to do it." He paused. "More likely, there's an object. Has the bride been gifted anything new?"

Bev snapped her fingers. "A bracelet. Marion gave it to her the day she arrived in town."

"That very well could be our cursed object," Percival said. "First things first, tell the bride to take off the bracelet. The more physical distance between her and it, the less the curse will affect her. If you bring it here, I *might* be able to break it. Depends on the complexity of the curse."

Bev's hopes soared. "Really? You'd do that for me?"

"Bev, you helped keep our town safe." Percival pointed to the amulet hanging from his neck. "Not to mention, you gave me my strength back. Whatever you need, I'm happy to provide."

The clock on the wall chimed. "I've got to get back," Bev said. "The wedding is this afternoon at four, and I'm sure the bride isn't going to be happy to give up her bracelet." She paused, glancing between the two. "If I can get it off her, could I send Lillie to bring it here?"

Percival tutted. "I'm still quite cross with her, gold and supplies aside. What she did—"

"Potentially did," Merv said.

"Oh, hush, you want more cookies," Percival chided gently. But when he turned back to Bev, he nodded. "For you, Bev. Yes. When I feel her cross the threshold, I'll come back and see what I can do to this bracelet to fix it."

Marion had cursed the wedding? She was pompous. Rude. Overbearing. And she clearly didn't think Allen was good enough for Vicky. But why would she go to the trouble of cursing the wedding when she seemed perfectly capable of undermining it in nonmagical ways?

It did explain why she'd been so intent on impressing Zed. Perhaps she thought if she kept his attention on her, he'd miss the magic she'd cast on the bride. That theory was a bit of a stretch, but it was still plausible.

She'd have to get the bracelet off Vicky and find the truth. She'd worry about the reason later.

The rain was starting to lessen, but the roads were certainly muddy and would make travel difficult. While most of those who were coming didn't live too far, and many lived in town, those traveling from Middleburg would face a difficult trek on sloppy roads. Especially wearing their finest attire.

"Come on, sun," Bev said, squinting at the sky. "Let's try to turn this around."

A few figures stood under the tent, pushing at the pockets of water with brooms. Karen was barking orders, and Bev's heart lightened when she recognized the other person.

"Grant!" Bev called, running toward the tent. "When did you get back in town?"

Grant turned and actually looked pleased to see Bev, which was a first for him. "Hey, Bev. Erm. Got in this morning. Left before dawn and walked back."

"And it's a good thing, too," Karen said, walking by. "Because we've still got to get your tunic altered."

"It's fine," Grant muttered, glaring at her. "Don't waste Apolinary's time on me. She's barely slept in days, so I hear."

"How is that dress coming?" Bev asked Karen. She'd been so busy with everything else, she'd completely forgotten about Apolinary toiling away on Vicky's dress.

"Should be about done, assuming there are no more problems," Karen said with a too-happy smile. "The weather is changing, the sun will come out, and today *will* be a beautiful wedding."

Bev couldn't help but notice the way she'd reached into her pocket, presumably to clutch that barus's bauble a little tightly.

"I'm headed to Apolinary's now to check on Vicky," Karen said. "Can I trust you to finish getting the rainwater off the tent, Grant?"

Bev looked up. There were still large droops in the top of the tent where the rainwater had gathered.

"Yep." He mock-saluted with the broom handle. "Will do."

Karen gave him a sideways glance before turning to Bev. "And shouldn't you be hard at work in the kitchen? We've got a crowd to feed. They're going to be mad if they come all this way and don't have anything to eat."

Before Bev could respond, Karen was ten steps away, talking to herself and ticking off her own list of tasks.

"She didn't get any less intense, did she?" Grant asked.

"No, she didn't. But she's not all bad." Bev turned to him. "I'm really glad to see you back, Grant. What changed your mind?"

He rubbed the back of his head. "PJ told me if I didn't come to my sister's wedding, he'd turn me into burnt toast, so…"

Bev smiled. "I know Vicky's going to be happy to see you."

"She won't if I'm the reason her wedding is ruined," he said, kicking the ground.

"It's not you," Bev said, putting her hand on his shoulder. "It's that blasted bracelet that Marion put on her. I think she cursed it."

"What?" Grant's gaze narrowed. "Why would she do that?"

"She doesn't want them to get married," Bev said. "She said so herself."

"Join the club," Grant muttered.

The clock in the town hall clanged, and Bev winced. She didn't have time to find Vicky; she was already behind schedule for the feast. As Karen had said, the crowd that was coming expected food.

"Listen," Bev said to Grant. "I've got a friend who might be able to undo the curse if we bring it to him. But I've got to get back to the inn. Do you think you can help?"

"I can try," he said with an emphatic nod. "I don't think she's going to give it up easily, though. Even if I tell her it's cursed."

Bev clicked her tongue. "Might want to keep that part close to the vest. I wouldn't want you to be on the wrong side of Allen's father."

He nodded. "So, figure a way to get my sister, who's obsessed with status, to take off the one piece of jewelry our pompous aunt gave her, without telling her it's cursed?" He snorted. "Easy as pie."

Chapter Twenty

Bev wished she could go with Grant to help, but the morning was getting away from her. She hurried back to the inn under an ominously dark sky. The front room of the inn was crowded with people, many of whom Bev didn't recognize. She had to assume they were distant relations who'd come in from Middleburg inns. The bespectacled man who'd shown up several days ago stood at the counter once more, wearing the same suit and intense look as Bev walked up.

"I'm here to witness the wedding of—"

"Yes, yes," Bev said with a smile. "It'll be at four o'clock this evening."

"Is the bride here?"

"Erm, I don't know where she is, exactly. Maybe at the seamstress shop," Bev said. "But I know she's quite busy, so—"

"Very well. Where is the wedding to take place? Here?"

"No," Bev said. "The town hall down the road. Big building. You can't miss it."

He nodded, picked up his briefcase, and walked out the door.

"Strange," Bev muttered.

"Bev!" Ida called from across the room. "Come take a look at our boy."

Allen stood in the corner in front of a mirror, presumably placed there by Apolinary sometime in the morning. He wore his wedding suit, a fancy tunic embroidered with gold. He looked uncomfortable, tugging at the collar and shifting from side to side. Beside him, Ida—wearing flowers in her hair—was adjusting the hem of his tunic and gazing at him as if he were a favorite brother.

Bev, too, took a moment to smile at him. Seeing him on his wedding day brought a warmth to her chest, and she couldn't help but go over to him. "Allen. You look so handsome."

He turned to her, looking like he was going to be sick. "This is insanity. This whole day keeps getting worse and worse."

"Oh, what's happened now?" Bev said.

"It's not a crisis," Ida said with a wave of her

hand. "Vellora's having some trouble finding a dry spot to start the fire for the pig. We'd obviously set up a tent before the rain started, but the high winds blew it down. But *don't worry*, Allen. This is the sort of thing that happens before a wedding. It'll be fine!"

Allen met Bev's gaze, concern evident on his face. "Bev, this isn't normal."

"No, it's not," Bev said, squeezing his shoulder. "But I think I've figured out what's happening. Should be fixed as soon as Grant—"

"Grant?" Allen frowned. "He's back?"

"Came back this morning." Bev beamed. "I told you he would."

"Yes, of course, after most of the work is done," Allen muttered then softened. "Vicky's going to be over the moon to see him. I'm glad he came to his senses."

"He's not the only one."

Jacob walked through the front door, removing a soaking-wet cloak that he hung on a peg near the door. Underneath, he wore an embroidered tunic similar to Allen's. The cousins stared at each other for a long moment before Jacob held out his hand.

"I'm sorry for what I said."

Allen glared at him and didn't take it. "I'm not sure you should've come back. Do you still think I shouldn't marry her?"

Jacob opened and closed his fist. It was clear his

opinion of the wedding hadn't changed, but he forced a smile. "You should do what makes you happy," he said with a long sigh. "And if this makes you happy, then…well, it can't be bad." He squeezed his cousin's shoulder. "Regardless, whatever decision you make, you're family. I'm going to be right there with you."

After a long pause, Allen reached up to cover his hand. "Thanks for coming back. Would've been weird to have Ida as my best woman."

"I would've done the job admirably," Ida said, puffing out her chest. "I've always wanted to be a best woman at a wedding."

"Next time," Bev said with a wink.

"You said things were fixed?" Allen said to Bev. "What did you do?"

"Not quite fixed yet, but they will be," Bev said. "I think I figured out who was behind all the mischief, too. Just can't figure the why." She shook her head. "But the important thing is that we'll get the curse broken—"

"Curse?" Jacob gave her a double take. "There's a *curse*?"

Allen turned to her, surprise on his face. "Like, a curse-curse?"

"What's this about curses?" Zed approached, earning an identical glare from Allen and Jacob. He looked between Allen and Bev before settling on the latter. "Tell me everything."

"Just a figure of speech," Bev said quickly with a thin smile. "I mean with all the catastrophes, really. Trying to lighten the mood, get everyone in a better frame of mind. There isn't a curse—"

Just then, a crack of lightning split the sky, and the windows rattled.

Bev cleared her throat and inched backward. "In any case, I've got to get into the kitchen. Don't want Karen to flay me for failing to provide for the guests. Allen, you're in good hands out here, right?"

"Why don't I help?" Jacob said, rolling up his sleeves. "It's the least I can do after disappearing all week."

"Glad to have it," Bev said. "Come on."

When she opened the door, Clarice was already seated on Bev's stool, peeling potatoes. The skins, of course, were being gobbled up by Biscuit before they hit the floor. Clarice had already peeled almost the entire bag and had Bev's schedule of events card sitting in front of her.

"Didn't know where you'd run off to, dear," Clarice said to Bev. "But I figured you wouldn't mind if I helped you get a head start."

"It's appreciated," Bev said, taking the card and checking the next task. "We'll need to start baking bread soon. I can only fit six of them at a time, so we'll need to start sooner rather than later. I've also got to roast an obscene amount of vegetables, peel and mash potatoes..." She paused. "Well, not peel.

Thank you for doing that."

"Of course."

"Where are the vegetables?" Jacob asked. "I'll get to chopping."

"In the root cellar," Bev said. "And if you'll grab me a couple of the breads in the tins, I'll get the oven—"

She turned, finally noticing the damp chill in the air. The ovens, which she'd started this morning, had gone out. She blew air between her lips and walked over, reaching inside to figure out what had gone wrong. The telltale feeling of dampness met her fingers.

"How did this get wet?" Bev muttered.

There wasn't time to worry about it, so Bev took a shovel and pulled all the wood and ash from the oven. She rushed down to her root cellar to fetch more firewood, and within ten minutes, a small fire was once again going in the oven. She brushed the top of her head, muttering to herself.

"C'mon, Grant. We need to get that bracelet off Vicky."

"What was that about Valeria?" Clarice asked.

"Nothing," Bev said, turning to the vegetables. She chopped faster than she ever had in her life, eyeing the card and the times. As long as she stuck to the schedule, everything would be fine. So far, things seemed back on track.

"Oh, *there* you are," Marion said, pushing open

the door. Lucy and Nadia followed. "Goodness me, I've been looking all over for you. For an innkeeper, you're quite derelict in your—"

"Yes, what can I help you with?" Bev said, her gaze on her knife as she chopped.

"Well, I was expecting a delivery of flowers this morning, and I haven't seen them yet. Tell me you didn't send away the delivery man?"

"Haven't seen a delivery man," Bev said. "Unless…he doesn't have glasses, does he?"

She laughed, the sound grating on Bev's already-frayed nerves. "How am I supposed to know that?"

"I sent him to the town hall," Bev said. "You might look for him there."

"In this weather?" Marion scoffed. "*Perfect* day for a wedding. We're going to be half-drowned walking down the street at this rate."

Bev tipped the vegetables into the pan and made a noise.

"Oh, surely, you aren't planning to cook such a simple dish for a wedding," Marion said, peering into the pan and scoffing. "Victoria requires elegance for her wedding—or as much as can be mustered in this town. Simple potatoes?"

"We're having to feed a crowd, so simplicity won," Bev said, leaning over the table and forcing a tight smile. "I think you three should go rest until this afternoon, eh? Or, if you'd like to be helpful, I'm sure there's plenty to do for Vicky, too."

"Oh, I wouldn't dream of going out there," Marion drawled. "Do you see all those people? I don't know half of them. Related to the baker, I imagine."

"Many of them are clients of the bride and groom," Jacob said. "Good for business to have them here."

"I see you've returned," Marion said, giving him a once-over. "Surprised Allen let you in the door. Running out as you did. Can't believe you'd leave your cousin in the lurch like that."

"Don't I recall you saying something similar?" Bev asked Marion. "You told the couple you didn't think they should get married."

Before she could answer, Wallace knocked on the kitchen door and walked in, gazing around as if looking for something.

"Erm, Bev," Wallace said. "Bit embarrassing, really. You haven't seen my holy book, have you?"

"No?" Bev frowned. "What does it look like?"

"Well, I'm *pretty* sure I brought it from Kaiser Tuckey's," he said with a sheepish grin. "Paul swears he saw me put it in my bag, but it's not there. I'm hoping maybe I left it in here? I don't remember bringing it to that counseling session, but perhaps I did."

Bev shook her head. "To my recollection, you had your notebook, but nothing else. I'm sure it'll turn up."

"Hope so," he said with a chuckle. "Can't marry the couple without it."

"You've got a spare, don't you?" Marion asked. "A cleric of your stature shouldn't carry around *one* holy book, should you?"

Before he could answer, the door opened *again*, and Karen stormed in with her usual intensity. "We need more vases. The wind came in and knocked over a table, and three of the flower vases broke."

"I don't have—"

"A tankard or glass will do," Karen said, a little impatiently. "I don't have time to argue, I—"

Before *she* could finish, Grant burst through the kitchen door, hunched over and panting. "Vicky's missing!"

Everyone in the kitchen stopped to look at him.

"What?" Karen said with a gasp.

"She was supposed to be at Apolinary's," he said, a little breathlessly. "She's not there. So I checked the bakery. Not there. I checked the Brewers' house. Not there. I checked the town hall, the tent, even the tea shop for good measure. Nowhere. And nobody's seen her all morning."

Bev turned to Karen, who licked her lips and reached into her pocket for the barus bauble.

"This…happens from time to time. Brides wander off. Run into someone, see someone they know, that sort of thing," Karen said with a nervous look. "I'll go find her."

She spun and headed not to the kitchen door, but to the front room. Bev, Marion, Lucy, Grant, and Wallace followed her as she walked up to Allen, who was still fussing with his tunic.

He spun, seeing the look on her face. "What's wrong now?" he asked.

"Erm. It seems Vicky isn't where she's supposed to be," Karen said, her voice quiet and her eyes filled with concern.

Allen frowned. "What do you mean?"

"I'm not saying she's—"

"She's missing," Grant said behind Karen. He rattled off the places he'd already looked. "And she's wearing that cursed bracelet."

"Grant," Bev muttered.

"Cursed?" Marion gasped, putting her hand to her chest. "Whatever do you mean?"

"So you do think there's a real curse." Zed had joined the gaggle around Allen. "If so, you need to tell me—"

"Let's put all that aside until we find Vicky," Bev said quickly. "Allen, where do you think she could be?"

Allen shook his head. "That's all the places I can think of. But maybe we should split up and look for her. I'm sure she's fine, but…" He shared a worried look with Bev. "Better to know she's safe."

Everyone, including—to Bev's surprise—

Marion, took a different part of town and set off immediately. Bev headed west out of town, Biscuit on her heels with his nose to the ground. They did a big loop, all the way to Alice's farm and beyond, and didn't find anything but Herman out inspecting his pumpkin vines.

They returned to town, Bev's pulse increasing as the time wore on. Forget dinner, how were they to have a wedding without a bride?

Biscuit scratched and pawed at the front door to the inn, and Bev let him in, trusting the laelaps knew more than she did. Inside, Marion was reading a book next to the fire. She seemed unbothered by the missing bride and the impending disaster, a thin smile adorning her lips.

"Oh, you're back," Marion said. "I haven't found those flowers I was looking for—"

"You're supposed to be looking for the bride," Bev said, a little hotly. "Or do you not care if Vicky shows up to her own wedding?"

"My dear, she *knows* where it is," Marion drawled. "She's the one who planned it, after all. If she doesn't show up, I suppose that will tell us if she wants to get married."

Bev glared at her. "Did you even try to look for her?"

"Of course I did," she said, brushing the hem of her skirt as she rose. "I checked three shops and didn't find her. Then I came back here to wait for the flower delivery man. I paid a lot of money for those flowers, and they—"

Bev glared at her. "Why in the world don't you want Vicky and Allen to get married?"

She blanched. "I'm sorry?"

"You told them it was a mistake," Bev said, her voice rising. "And you gave Vicky that cursed bracelet—"

"What in the world are you talking about?" Marion said. "Cursed? It's magnificent. A family heirloom. She should be grateful I hung onto it all these years."

"And full of evil magic designed to ruin Vicky's wedding," Bev said. "What was the point? You couldn't stand for someone else to have a nice wedding? Have something against Vicky's mother? Or are you so mean-spirited that you'd ruin a perfectly nice couple's wedding for the fun of it?"

Marion's gaze narrowed. "I have *no idea* what you're talking about."

"Someone has placed a curse on this wedding," Bev enunciated slowly. "A real curse. Magic. And I've got a hunch that bracelet has something to do with it."

Marion cleared her throat. "Well, if the wedding is cursed, don't blame me. I certainly don't dabble in *that sort* of magic. Do you have any idea how much a spell like that would cost a person these days? And for what? So my country niece's wedding would be ruined? I'm aghast you think me so cruel."

Bev hesitated. She certainly sounded sincere. "Well, if it wasn't you, then who was it? And why?"

"Excuse me."

Mr. Morley was back. Bev pinched the bridge of her nose. "The wedding hasn't begun yet. Go to the town—"

"Yes, I'm quite aware. Four o'clock. Town hall." He placed his briefcase on the table. "I was hoping to see the bride before, as we have paperwork to attend to."

"What kind of paperwork?" Marion said. "And who are you? Some kind of wedding licenser?"

"My name is Duckett Morley," he said, giving her a once-over. "I'm coming from the First Royal Bank in Sheepsburg. I've been informed that Ms. Victoria Hamblin of Pigsend will be wedded to Mr. Allen Mackey this day, which effectively satisfies the requirements for her inheritance."

Chapter Twenty~One

"Inheritance?" Marion looked as dumbfounded as Bev. "Victoria doesn't have an inheritance that I'm aware of."

"Indeed she does." He pulled a sheet of paper from his briefcase and read. "It is hereby noted that Griselda Hamblin's estate will be kept in suspension until such time that her eldest daughter, Victoria, reaches the age of twenty-one. If, at twenty-one, the eldest is still unmarried, the account shall be transferred to the custodian." He rolled up the paper and put it back in his briefcase. "Ergo, I'm here to confirm that she will, in fact, be married so that we can begin the process of delivering her funds, as instructed."

Marion snatched the paper from him, reading it several times, then her hand came to her mouth. "Lucy."

"What?" Bev took a step forward. "What about Lucy?"

"That conniving little…" Marion balled the paper, earning a cry of surprise from Mr. Morley, who took it from her and smoothed it out gently. "I was…out of town when Mama passed. Lucy said she would handle everything, and to my eyes, it was handled. I thought… well, Lucy *told* me Mama had cut Griselda out of the will. You know, because she married—"

"The farmhand." Vicky's grandmother sounded like a piece of work. "But she didn't?"

"This is exactly the amount of money I inherited from my mother's estate. I don't think Griselda had any money of her own when she passed, so this must be Griselda's share of our mother's money." Marion looked at Mr. Morley. "You said if Vicky doesn't marry by her twenty-first birthday, the money goes to the custodian?"

"The instructions are quite clear," he said. "So where's the bride?"

"We're looking for her," Bev said. "Marion, did Lucy—?"

She nodded. "She had the bracelet. She *suggested* that I give it to Vicky. I can't *believe* she would do this."

"We have to find your sister," Bev said.

"Stay here, Mr. Morley," Marion said. "We'll be back with some answers."

~

Of all people, Bev wouldn't have guessed she'd be running through the muddy streets with Marion. The discovery of the inheritance had stripped the elder woman of all her bravado, leaving her cursing her sister's name and angry with herself for not seeing it sooner.

"How much is this inheritance?" Bev asked Marion as they checked inside every store for Lucy.

"If it's the same as what I inherited," Marion said, "then it's quite a large sum, indeed. Life-changing."

"And you had no idea this money had been set aside?" Bev asked.

She slowed. "I perhaps should've been more persistent in my investigation. But I assumed, you know. Mama was so angry with Griselda for leaving the way she did. She was betrothed to another man when she skipped town with the farmhand, and it was such the scandal."

"Is that why you never reached out to help Vicky after her father passed?"

"It's not my finest moment," Marion said, with a rare bit of humility. "I, too, was hurt that her mother decided a farmhand was better company than us. She told us as much, too, which didn't help things. And I supposed I figured if I closed my eyes, the two children weren't my problem." She shook her head. "But this? Keeping their inheritance from them isn't right."

In the middle of town, they found Karen and Grant, and told them what was going on. Grant's face went beet-red at the news, and Karen's eyes narrowed so hard they almost disappeared.

"That perfidious—"

"Save your names for when we find her," Bev said.

They compared notes and were able to narrow places in town where neither Vicky nor Lucy were. There weren't many places left, but Biscuit came running down the street, barking at Bev.

"Follow that laelaps," Bev cried, turning to run beside him.

He led the group back to the inn but didn't stop in the front room. Bev followed him up the stairs, taking them two at a time, with Marion, Grant, and Karen hot on her heels. Biscuit scampered down the hall and pawed at room one, and Bev didn't even wait before flinging open the door.

Lucy was sitting on her bed, the content smile disappearing from her face as soon as the door opened. "What's happened? Did you find Vicky? Is she all right?"

"We haven't found her yet," Bev said. "But somehow I don't think you'll mind that too much."

Lucy laughed nervously, her gaze sweeping from person to person. "What do you mean?"

"You cursed Vicky," Marion said. "Mr. Morley, from the First Royal Bank, is downstairs. He says he's here to witness the wedding of Vicky and Allen so he can signify she's eligible to receive her inheritance."

Lucy, to her credit, looked confused, although the tone of her voice was a bit higher than it should've been. "What inheritance?"

"The one you've been keeping from us," Grant snarled, pushing past Karen. "How could you? We've been here struggling—"

"If you struggled, you can blame your mother," Lucy said. "It's not our job to keep a pair of farmhand children fed and clothed. She had a perfect life in Sheepsburg and threw it all away, and the rest of us were left to deal with the consequences."

Bev couldn't help but notice the *anger* in her voice. It seemed personal. "It's about more than the money, isn't it?" Bev turned to Marion. "You said Vicky's mother was engaged before she left, right?"

"To a family friend," Marion said, before a light came into her eyes. She seemed to see her sister for the first time. "You loved him, too, didn't you?"

Lucy nodded, hurt filling her eyes. "And he wanted nothing to do with our family after that. He was the man *I* wanted to marry, but he only had eyes for Griselda. When she left..." She shook her head.

"You can't punish the children for the pain their mother caused you," Bev said, after a long pause. "And you certainly shouldn't have *cursed* Vicky and Allen."

"Did them a favor!" Lucy cried. "They've done nothing but bicker and argue and snap at each other. Never seen a couple more ill-suited for marriage than them."

"And in three months, when Vicky turns twenty-one and she's not married, you'll collect a few thousand gold coins, won't you?" Grant said.

"A few thousand? My dear, it's probably close to thirty thousand gold coins," Marion said with a wave of her hand.

The color left the teen's face as he turned to his aunt in shock.

"It's not up to you to say whether they should get married or not," Bev said. "Now, did you curse the bracelet?"

Lucy licked her lips and didn't respond for a few moments. But finally, she gave a clipped, "Yes."

"Great, now we need to find Vicky, and—"

"Erm? Are you looking for Vicky?" Zed called from the bottom of the stairs. "Because she and Allen just walked through the door."

⁓

Vicky and Allen stood in the front room,

looking quite sheepish. Vicky wore her regular clothes, her hair brushed, but not decorated. Allen's shirt was muddy, and Bev could only imagine Karen's annoyance at the state of it.

"Oh, thank heavens!" Karen said, her hand coming to her chest as she brushed past Bev to run to the bride. "Vicky, goodness me, you gave us a fright!"

"I'm so sorry," Vicky said softly. "I just… I needed some space to think."

"Think about what?" Bev asked.

"Erm, we have an announcement," Vicky said softly.

"You're having a baby?" Clarice called from the kitchen. Bev had forgotten she and Jacob were still putting together the feast.

"No," Allen said with a glare. "No, we've decided…"

Vicky swallowed hard. "We've decided to call off the wedding."

Nobody spoke for a moment.

"Call it off?" Bev said softly. "Are you sure?"

"Surer now than ever," Vicky said, sharing a look with Allen. "When I woke up this morning, I had the strongest feeling that I shouldn't do this. That I was making a big mistake, and if I walk down the aisle—"

"That's because your *aunt* levied a curse on your wedding," Marion said, snarling at Lucy. "Take off that bracelet, and we'll see how you truly feel."

Vicky blinked. "I'm sorry, what?"

"Just take off the bracelet," Bev said, stepping forward and holding out her hand. "And then see how you feel."

With a sideways look at Bev, Vicky reached down to unclasp the bracelet and put it in Bev's hand.

Bev turned to glare at Lucy. "Well? Is she still cursed?"

"Yes," Lucy said through gritted teeth. "Until we can get it to a cursebreaker—"

"I've got it." Zed strode forward, pulling a vial from his pocket. "When Bev said that the wedding was cursed earlier, I fetched this vial from my room. It's a potion that helps destroy magic. Quite useful in my line of work, you know." He held out his hand. "Give it to me."

Bev handed it over and held her breath as he poured the potion over the diamonds. They hissed and crackled and popped, then it stopped. The bracelet looked exactly the same, but the vice that had been around Bev's chest for the past few days eased.

"There," Zed said with a smile, handing the bracelet back to Vicky. "All fixed. No more curse."

"Well?" Bev asked. "Do you still want to call off the wedding?"

Vicky looked at Allen, who smiled back at her.

Then, they both started laughing.

"Oh, absolutely yes," Vicky said, turning to the group with a wide smile. "This has been the worst week of my life."

"But it was the curse!" Marion said.

"And if we were right for one another," Allen said, "the curse should've made us stronger. We should've been a team. Instead, all we did was argue and complain and gripe at one another." He squeezed Vicky's hand. "Wallace told us this wedding was going to be the least of the challenges we face. And if we can't even get through a single ceremony without losing it, what hope do we have of a life together?"

"I think that's very wise," Marion said softly.

"Apolinary's going to kill me," Vicky said, putting her hand to her head. "She's been bending over backward to make this wedding gown, and—"

"Not to mention Lillie," Allen said with a groan. "And everyone who traveled—"

"Am I to understand that you will not be getting married, Ms. Hamblin?" Mr. Morley had witnessed the whole thing, standing off to the side with his briefcase in hand.

"Who are you?" Vicky asked.

"He's the man who's got the keys to our inheritance," Grant said.

Vicky spun around, shock evident on her face. "What? What inheritance?"

Mr. Morley sighed loudly as he pulled out the sheet of paper again. "It is hereby noted that Griselda Hamblin's estate will be kept in suspension until such time that her eldest daughter, Victoria, reaches the age of twenty-one. If, at twenty-one, the eldest is still unmarried, the account shall be transferred to the custodian."

"The custodian being Lucy Edelbert," Bev finished.

Vicky stared at Allen wordlessly. "How much are we talking?"

"Enough that you don't want to let it go," Marion said. "Trust me. You and your brother wouldn't have to work again in your lives."

Vicky swayed slightly as she looked at Grant, who watched her with bated breath. "And in order to inherit this life-changing sum, Allen and I have to marry?" she asked softly.

"If it means you'll get the money that's rightfully yours," Allen nodded firmly, "I'd marry you every day."

She smiled at him, but there wasn't much happiness in it. "Then I suppose we'd better head to the town hall."

"Vicky," Marion said, sounding gentler than she ever had before, "I want to offer you a deal."

Vicky looked up at her, confused.

"I confess, I had *no* idea about this…*stipulation*. I honestly didn't even *know* there was money left in your mother's accounts." She cast a derisive look toward her sister. "And I'm *furious* that you would keep that from me, Lucy. Keep that from these two children. Goodness knows they've had a rough go of it."

"What's your deal?" Vicky asked, a little impatiently.

"If you agree to *not* marry this very nice man you clearly don't want to marry," Marion said. "I will make sure this inheritance is fairly delivered to you and your brother, the way it *should've* been." She sent another glare to her sister.

"But what about the marriage stipulation?" Vicky asked, looking at Mr. Morley.

"My good sir," Marion said with a look so sharp it could've peeled the skin off a potato. "You work for Mr. Parma there at the First Royal Bank, do you not?"

"He's the owner of the bank, yes—"

"Mr. Parma and I are on a first-name basis, you know. And as the *current* matriarch of the Edelbert clan, I do have some say about how the estate should be handled."

"Erm, no, you…" He wilted under her stare. "I'm sure we can figure something out."

"There." Marion turned to Vicky with a smile. "Well, Vicky?"

Vicky looked at Allen, who held her hand tightly. "We spent so much money," she said with a low laugh. "I feel awful—"

"Don't." Allen squeezed her hand. "I'd rather you go off and enjoy your life. Have adventures. You deserve it. And I've increased my client base tenfold, so maybe it'll pay off..." He laughed, a little forlornly. "Eventually."

"I also have something to say." Zed strode forward. "First, I want to say that I fully support you two going your separate ways. I'm sure there's a way we can adjust the will so the money goes where it's supposed to. *If only because* it seems the current custodian won't be around to collect it."

All the color left Lucy's face.

"But before I get to that," Zed said, turning to Allen. "Upstairs in my room, there's a large sack of coins I've been saving for you. It's not quite as much as your former bride's inheritance, but it's enough." He smiled at Allen, who stared back slack-jawed. "I'd hoped to give it to you at the reception tonight, but it seems your happy ending may lie elsewhere."

"I don't know what to..." Allen swallowed. "Thank you."

"It doesn't make up for the time I was gone," he said, squeezing Allen's shoulder. "But it's a start." He turned to Lucy, the warmth evaporating from his face. "Ms. Edelbert, why don't we take a walk? Seems like we have a lot to discuss."

"I'll go with you," Marion said, taking her sister's arm with perhaps more force than was necessary. "Because I *also* have a lot to discuss with my sister."

But before the trio could depart, Karen let out a wail. "*What am I going to do?* This was supposed to be my last chance! I'm out of money, out of ideas, and I don't have a single client waiting for me in Middleburg!" She fell to her knees, crying into her hands.

"It seems to me, Ms. Mayhew, that you should pull yourself together," Marion said, standing by the door. "We may not have a wedding today, but we certainly will be having a party, and a few hundred hungry people. I suggest everyone gets to work so we don't have to disappoint them twice."

And with that, she strolled out the door with Zed and Lucy.

"Well, you heard the woman," Bev said with a laugh. "We've got one heck of a party to throw tonight. To the not-wedding of Vicky and Allen! Break out the wine!"

Chapter Twenty~Two

In the history of Pigsend parties, the not-wedding was certainly one for the record books. Nearly two hundred people attended, including every farmer from Pigsend and the surrounding areas. There was a bit of confusion about why Vicky and Allen weren't getting married, but it turned out there was a couple who could stand in their place.

"It would be criminal to let all this good work go to waste," Etheldra said, turning to Earl. "Well?"

"Well, what?" he said with a blank look.

"Men." She shook her head. "Meet me up front at four. I've got to go find a dress. Maybe I can squeeze into Vicky's."

Wallace was pleased as punch to wed the elderly

couple. Although he said it was a bit unorthodox for him to marry them without counseling first, he had a good feeling that neither party was walking into this without having thought about it.

The sky had cleared to a beautiful vibrant blue, the warm sun soaked up the water on the roads, and everyone was in great spirits. The town was as busy as during the annual Harvest Festival, and by the time Bev finished cooking all the food, there wasn't a seat to be had in the town hall.

At four on the nose, Etheldra showed up in Vicky's remade dress, which did, in fact, fit her quite nicely. Ida, being Etheldra's only living relative, was pleased as punch to be the best man, while Jane Medlam, the mason, stood beside her carpenter friend. Etheldra lingered by the front door, Vicky's bouquet in her hand, and for a moment, Bev worried the older woman might be getting cold feet.

"What are you waiting on?" Shasta Brewer, who stood by the door, whispered to Etheldra.

"For Bev to get over here and walk me," Etheldra said, her sharp voice booming across the hall.

All eyes swept to Bev, and she about jumped out of her skin. She wanted to argue, but she'd long learned that arguing with Etheldra Daws a losing proposition. So she adjusted her tunic, wishing she'd worn something that didn't have blotches of flour on it, and stepped up to take the other woman's arm.

"Thank you," Etheldra said. "Since, other than Earl, you're the one I like the best in this town."

Bev's heart swelled as she escorted the other woman, and it was about ready to burst as they drew closer to Earl, whose eyes shone with tears. Bev swallowed hard as she offered Etheldra's arm then stepped back to stand next to Ida, who was full-on crying. The butcher grasped Bev's arm with a little more force than necessary.

"Welcome," Wallace boomed to the crowd. "This isn't the most conventional wedding I've ever been a part of, but I'm glad you're here. And I'm even more glad that Vicky and Allen stepped aside so these two...*young* lovebirds could make their vows known."

Allen and Vicky, seated in the front row, stood and waved at the crowd, who, thanks to the grapevine that was Pigsend, already knew all the sordid details about the curse.

Wallace then turned to the couple before him to continue the ceremony. Earl spoke tearfully about how much Etheldra meant to him, and Etheldra even had some nice words to say about Earl, which didn't leave a dry eye in the town hall. Even Mayor Hendry, watching from her office doorway, wiped away a tear.

As the ceremony drew to a close, Wallace

declared them husband and wife then turned to the crowd to introduce the couple. "It gives me great pleasure to introduce Mr. and Mrs—"

"If you call me Mrs. Earl Dollman, I will gut you," Etheldra said with a look.

"Erm. Mrs. Etheldra Daws and Mr. Earl Dollman!"

The crowd, many of whom loved Earl as much as Vicky and Allen (and had a nervous respect for Etheldra), cheered wildly. Then they filed out of the town hall into the garland-covered wedding tent. Apparently, all the rain had caused a burst of new flowers in the fields outside town, and Vicky was able to remake her arrangements. She was happier than Bev had ever seen her, laughing brightly with the Brewer twins and Nadia, who even looked to be in a better mood.

Allen, too, was overjoyed, the stress and tension that had been on his face for weeks now completely gone. The Witzels took turns making fun of him for canceling his own wedding then hugged him tightly and kissed his cheeks. Jacob and Clarice, who'd helped Bev get over the finish line with the food, were all smiles, too.

"I knew he'd come to his senses," Clarice said, as Biscuit sat by her side, wagging his tail. "I had a feeling everything would work out in the end. These things do, you know."

Vellora had been able to find a dry spot to cook

the pig, which was served up on a platter in the center of the tent. Bev's side dishes paired up nicely, and some of the farmers had brought in fresh fruits and vegetables to accompany the meal. All in all, it was an absolute feast for the crowd, and before long, all of it was eaten.

"Well done, Vellora," Bev said with an approving nod after finishing her fill. "Truly, you're a master at the grill pit."

"Suppose I'd better keep the pit ready for the solstice," she said. "Because, erm, my commander said he was going to plan a visit. Said my letter intrigued him."

Bev nodded lightly, not sure how she wanted to react to that news and the idea that more of her past might be uncovered in the coming weeks. "I see. Well, I'll be sure to keep a place for him at the inn."

Next, it was time for the newlywed couple to share a dance, thanks to the band of farmers Vicky had hired to play. Bev hadn't a clue that Dane Sterling, Eldred Nest, and the miller Sonny Gray were so musically inclined, but they filled the tent with loud guitar strummings and flutes that put everyone in a good mood. Once their slow waltz concluded, and all the tables were rolled away, the tent became the largest party hall Bev had ever been in. Not one for dancing herself, she didn't have a choice as Ida pulled her to the center for a complicated dance that everyone in Pigsend seemed to know by heart. After that was another waltz, and Bev couldn't get out of dancing with the groom. Then, another fast one, and Bev joined in a circle with Vicky, Apolinary (who was overjoyed Vicky had called off the wedding), and the Brewer twins.

The sun set, and the tent was illuminated by a hundred candles. Bev could only imagine what might've happened to those candles if the curse had still been in effect. But the night was as perfect as could be expected, almost a balance to the calamities caused by the curse.

Balance. Percival had once said magic required balance. Was this the backlash of the curse? Perfect luck?

The planner was in her element, running around and directing guests as if she were a general commanding an army. She barely had time to acknowledge Bev as she ran by but did give her a small smile. Karen paused, only briefly, to bid hello to Marion and Zed, neither of whom seemed happy to be back in the tent. But after a few moments, they visibly relaxed, leaving Bev to wonder what they'd done with Lucy.

When the band stopped playing, Allen and Lillie brought out the cake to raucous cheers. Bev couldn't help but be impressed. It was the same five tiers as the original cake, covered in white icing, and the delicate piping on top was exquisite. Allen stepped back to let Lillie soak in the moment. She looked exhausted, but waved happily to the crowd, tears in her eyes, then stepped aside as Etheldra and Earl came up to cut the cake.

"I have high expectations for this," Etheldra said to Lillie.

They sliced together, revealing a beautiful yellow sponge, which Etheldra declared to be the best lemon cake she'd had in her life. Lillie's cheeks went pink as Allen shooed her away so he could serve cake to the crowd.

Lillie joined Bev off to the side and took her hands. "What a week!"

"Welcome to Pigsend," Bev said with a laugh. "You really did great on that cake, Lillie. It's magnificent."

"Skin of my teeth, that's what that was," she said with a loud sigh. Her gaze shifted around, perhaps looking for Zed. "Had to use every trick in my arsenal to get the sponges cool enough to ice and decorate. But here we are. Done." She laughed. "And not even for Allen's wedding!" She smiled at Earl and Etheldra, who were enjoying the fruits of her labor. "But I suppose it doesn't matter. As long as it's delicious."

"Lillie, you outdid yourself!" Vicky said, walking over with a slice, which she handed to Bev. "Everything is so perfect. I couldn't have been happier with how it all came out."

Bev laughed. "Even though you weren't the

bride?"

"You know," Karen said with an appraising look at Vicky, "I think you have the makings of an amazing event planner."

Vicky barked a laugh. "If this is what you do every day, I don't think I can handle it. This one about took me out." She smiled at Karen. "Are you… Are you going to be all right?"

"I'm *better* than all right," Karen said. "Your aunt Marion has already hired me for her solstice party this winter, and she says she has three friends with major birthdays this fall. I'd planned on starting my business in Middleburg, but it seems Sheepsburg is going to be my new home for a while." She let out a sigh. "Thank you, Vicky, for having the worst wedding I've ever managed."

Vicky laughed. "I'm so happy I could be of service."

"What about you?" Lillie asked Vicky. "What are your plans?"

Vicky's smile faded a little. "I'm leaving with Marion tomorrow for Sheepsburg as well. We've got to sort out this inheritance mess, but she's positive she can bully someone into changing things. In the meantime, she's given me and Grant an advance of three hundred gold coins, to get us on our feet."

"That's awfully nice of her," Bev said. "I know Grant could use the money. Is he coming with you?"

Vicky shook her head. "He said he'd already

plotted how he was going to make his own way, whatever that means, and that I wasn't to worry about him. Of course, I'm going to, but with this money, he can stay in the apartment above Apolinary's shop." She smiled. "Will you keep an eye on him for me, Bev?"

"We all will," Bev said.

"I think he wants to stay with his friends," Vicky said. "He's pretty attached to PJ Norris. He said he needed to stick around to make sure he doesn't get into trouble. I don't know what that means, but..."

Bev did. "You've got a good brother, Vicky."

Vicky softened, watching him in the corner with PJ and Valta. "Yeah, I do. Can you imagine he thought he was the reason for the curse?" She scowled and shook her head. "Can't believe that Lucy. All because she was jealous my mother didn't want to marry the man she wanted."

"Love makes people do silly things," Bev said, watching Earl and Etheldra waltz along the center of town. "Look at them. Can't believe they're married."

"Finally." Ida walked up to Bev and threw an arm around her. "We've all been waiting for them to tie the knot for *ages*."

"Don't suppose it's going to make her less..." Vicky said with a look.

The group let out a laugh.

"Never," Bev said. "She is who she is."

With the cake cut and the toasts made, the only thing left to do was get back to dancing. Once again, Bev was pulled this way and that, made to perform dances she had no hope of keeping up with. But she was happy to be there, and overjoyed that once again, there was peace in Pigsend.

As the event drew to a close, she found herself standing next to Zed, who had a goblet of wine and was watching Allen and Vicky dance without a care in the world.

"Suppose it's for the best," Zed said to Bev as he nodded to his son. "Maybe they'll find their way back to one another one day."

"Maybe," Bev said. She eyed him. "Where's Lucy?"

"Let's not talk about unpleasant things," Zed said. "It's my son's not-wedding day. And Etheldra and Earl, who'd have thought? They were always sniping at each other when I was younger." He smiled. "Suppose the trip was worth it, if only to see Etheldra finally settle down."

"It's pretty convenient you had that potion," Bev said, still not fully convinced Zed was here for the wedding alone.

"Standard issue," he said.

"What kind of potion is it?" Bev asked. "One that can dissolve magic?"

"Kind of," he said. "You can't really dissolve

magic, but you can make an object forget that they have it."

Bev shifted. "What?" Then, sensing Zed's curiosity, she cleared her throat. "I mean, what do you mean by that?"

"Well, magic clings to an object because the object remembers, not because the magic is sticky, and none so sticky as a curse. So, if one doesn't have a cursebreaker handy, one can usually break the spell by making the cursed object forget it's been cursed."

Bev nodded, unable to stop herself from asking, "And what would happen if a *person* with magic ingested that potion?"

"Hm. I'm not sure." He turned to her. "Why do you ask?"

His stare was piercing, and Bev could practically hear his thoughts.

"If you want my advice, Bev," he said when she didn't respond, "the past is the past. And as long as you stay out of magical trouble in the future, you should have no quarrel with Her Majesty's forces."

Vellora waltzed by with Ida, and Bev swallowed hard. Magical trouble, it seemed, would be coming whether she wanted it to or not.

Bev continues her adventures in

ZEALOTS AND ZENITHS

Weary Dragon Inn

BOOK SEVEN

Acknowlegments

As always, first thanks goes to my husband for believing in me and for managing the toddler in the evenings. Thanks, also, go to my son, for continuing to insist upon his six o'clock bedtime so I could write yet another book in the dark. Shout-out to Ms. Rachel, too. You're the real MVP.

Thanks to Chelsea, Danielle, and Lisa for being the all-star team who helps keep me going. And to my writer pals, Brett, Kelsey, and Emily, for keeping me sane.

Also By the Author

The Princess Vigilante Series

Brynna has been protecting her kingdom as a masked vigilante until one night, she's captured by the king's guards. Instead of arresting her, the captain tells her that her father and brother have been assassinated and she must hang up her mask and become queen.

The Princess Vigilante series is a four-book young adult epic fantasy series, perfect for fans of Throne of Glass and Graceling.

The Seod Croí Chronicles

After her father's murder, princess Ayla is set to take the throne — but to succeed, she needs the magical stone her evil stepmother stole. Fortunately, wizard apprentice Cade and knight Ward are both eager to win Ayla's favor.

A Quest of Blood and Stone is the first book in the *Seod Croí* chronicles and is available now in eBook, paperback, and hardcover.

Also By the Author

The Madion War Trilogy

He's a prince, she's a pilot, they're at war. But when they are marooned on a deserted island hundreds of miles from either nation, they must set aside their differences and work together if they want to survive.

The Madion War Trilogy is a fantasy romance available now in eBook, Paperback, and Hardcover.

empath

Lauren Dailey is in break-up hell, but if you ask her she's doing just great. She hears a mysterious voice promising an easy escape from her problems and finds herself in a brand new world where she has the power to feel what others are feeling. Just one problem—there's a dragon in the mountains that happens to eat Empaths. And it might be the source of the mysterious voice tempting her deeper into her own darkness.

Empath is a stand-alone fantasy that is available now in eBook, Paperback, and Hardcover.

About the Author

S. Usher Evans was born and raised in Pensacola, Florida. After a decade of fighting bureaucratic battles as an IT consultant in Washington, DC, she suffered a massive quarter-life-crisis. She found fighting dragons was more fun than writing policy, so she moved back to Pensacola to write books full-time. She currently resides there with her husband and kids, and frequently can be found plotting on the beach.

Visit S. Usher Evans online at:
http://www.susherevans.com/